Jeanine has nowhere left to turn but to God.

Colbert had taken his place with the bishop, and Jeanine refused to give in to the look of triumph upon his face. God would save her. Whether it be in the midst of flames as He took her spirit up to heaven, or in the miraculous rescue that Victor had promised.

The priest again appeared below her to offer up prayers on her behalf. Jeanine felt desperation edging out her confidence. *I can do this,* she promised herself. *I can stand strong in the face of this false accusation because God knows my innocence.* She took a deep breath and caught the priest's sympathetic expression.

"What of my parents?" Jeanine dared to ask.

The priest shrugged. "It is better this way, *non?* 'Twould be difficult for them to observe their child burned alive."

Jeanine swallowed hard. Victor and Étienne had promised to return, but there was no sign of them or anyone else who might offer her love in her final moments. Sweat formed on her brow, and her stomach churned with revolting anxiety.

"Let us finish this thing," Colbert called out. "The sun is now in the sky."

Five Geese Flying

Tracie Peterson

Heartsong Presents

A note from the Author:
*I love to hear from my readers! You may correspond
with me by writing:*

**Tracie Peterson
Author Relations
P.O. Box 719
Uhrichsville, OH 44683**

ISBN 1-57748-271-9

FIVE GEESE FLYING

Cover illustration by Lorraine Bush.

PRINTED IN THE U.S.A.

one

1390
Bruges, Flanders—France

"The arrangement has been that you would cancel all debts accrued over the last five years," François de la Fontaine reminded his opponent. And indeed, it seemed that the two men were squaring off for a battle rather than arranging a marriage.

Jeanine de la Fontaine watched the entire ordeal from the hearthside, where she continued to spin wool with her distaff until her fingers felt as though they would bleed at any moment. How could her father just give her over to Antoine Colbert? The man was hideous and nearly twice her age. His greasy blond hair hung matted around his balding head, only to be awkwardly accompanied by an equally matted beard. It was as if God had taken the hair from his head to put it on the man's face.

Jeanine shuddered and continued to listen to her father's bartering. Before the night was out, she would be the betrothed of Antoine Colbert, and there was nothing she could do about it.

" 'Tis true enough that I have agreed to such an arrangement in the past," Antoine was saying, "but, I did not chance to imagine the depths to which you would plunge into debt."

"You know well enough, milord, the River Zwin is filling with silt. It makes trade difficult at best. Two of my finest ships were grounded with entire sections of the hull torn away. It made repairs costly and difficult. Some of the cargo was lost to us, but the remainder should bring a fair price."

"Aye, but what will you do for trade when the river closes altogether? How then will you pay me rent and taxes?"

"I'll trust the Lord God to provide at that turn," Jeanine's father replied.

Antoine Colbert laughed heartily, and Jeanine watched as his rotund, overfed belly shook in maniacal delight. "If the Lord God cared that much, Fontaine, mayhap He should have had the foresight to keep the river from filling in the first place."

"Talk not in such a manner against our Lord," her father answered angrily. "Our house is one that serves Him first. You may own a portion of this village—indeed, you may believe you own me—but I am God's servant."

Jeanine glanced up to make out the tightened features of her father's face. He was only forty years old, but he looked half again as many years. His face was etched with worry lines that made Jeanine fear for his health. Her mother took this moment of tension to bring drinks and bread to the table. Jeanine watched as her mother gently brushed her father's shoulder while Colbert dug into the refreshments. Margarite de la Fontaine knew how to soothe her husband with a simple touch. Jeanine watched as the anger washed from her father's face.

It appeared to Jeanine that Colbert would see the unity as a threat and maybe even a defeat. His countenance changed as though he were considering exactly how far he could push this family. He cast a glance to Jeanine and caught her watching him before she could look away. Her body shuddered at the thought of marriage, and Colbert grinned wickedly as if reading those thoughts for himself.

Colbert squared his shoulders and looked her father in

the eye. "You drive a hard bargain, François, but I will honor my word. After all, what be a man, but that which is his word—eh?"

Jeanine saw her father nod hesitantly. "And you will cancel out the entire five years?"

"Aye," Colbert replied, returning his gaze to Jeanine. "She appears well worth the debt. Her hands are swift to create as she has proven with her woolens. She is sound of mind, which makes the arrangement twice the bargain. I fear the madness of poverty and plague has left many a young woman addlepated. Her skin is not pox marked and scarred. Neither is it of ill pallor. Aye, she will warm my bed well and give me many strong sons. Five years debt seems a mere pittance."

Jeanine wanted to club the smirking man over the head. He treated her as though she were a brood mare being purchased off the block. If she'd had less love and respect for her father, she might have protested and declared her disgust with the entire arrangement. Her mother and father had married out of arrangement as well, but they had also loved each other and thus found such matters completely acceptable. Their arranged marriage bore little resemblance to the marriage that awaited Jeanine. Antoine Colbert was notorious for his filthy habits and perversions. That her father had found himself helpless against this man sorrowed her deeply. That he found it necessary to give her over in barter to him left her angry and frightened.

"I will have the contracts drawn," Colbert said, pushing back from the table. His chair went tumbling over backward and crashed against the wooden plank floor. "I suggest an immediate union."

Jeanine could stand it no longer. "I beg you, Father, pray give me time to arrange myself for such an alteration in my life. There is much to be done before I can leave your house and become the wife of Monsieur Colbert."

"You are a woman a full score in years," Colbert replied haughtily. "Methinks after twenty years there cannot be much in the way of preparation yet undone. Surely your life has been given over to learning the proper skills to be pleasing to a husband."

Jeanine felt her face flush and was grateful for the nearness of the fire. Perhaps no one would notice in the dim light of the room, but should they see her flushed, 'twould be fitting they blame the warmth of the hearth and not her anger.

"My mother has trained me in the services necessary to the keeping of a household, I assure you." Jeanine folded her hands demurely in her lap and turned a hopeful expression on her father. "Please, *Père*. I beg you give me but a short time to complete my preparations. I've not yet created a gown in which to be married."

Her father's expression turned tender. "I suggest six weeks from this day would give the child enough time," he said, turning to face Colbert.

The man looked as though he might argue the point, then gave a stiff bow and nodded. "Very well. That will put us well out of the Lenten season. There should be no further cause for delay after that."

Jeanine rose and curtseyed. "You are most gracious, milord." She barely choked the words out from between clenched teeth. There was nothing gracious about the man. He was an unmitigated boar and a self-centered pig.

Colbert left with the promise that he would return when the contract had been put to paper. The door to the de la Fontaine house was scarcely closed behind him, when Jeanine's father sat down heavily and put his head in his hands.

"Why did you risk bringing his ire down upon this

house, *ma petite angée?*"

"I'm no angel, Father. I could not bear the man's stench, much less the idea of becoming his wife," Jeanine declared. "I cannot see why this arrangement must include me as the solution." She tossed her distaff aside. "I did not want to show disrespect to you in front of him, but how can you expect me to marry him? He's grotesque, and you know his reputation. 'Tis one that suggests much misery and horror."

Her father raised his head and regarded her for a moment. When he answered her, he spoke in a tone of total defeat. "You will do as you are told. 'Tis not my way, but that which must be done, will be done."

She opened her mouth as if to rage at the injustice of it all, but she could see the pain on her father's face. She knew that her beloved *père* would not have forced her into this marriage had the circumstances not been severe. She left her place by the fire and came to stand beside her father. "*Oui.* I will do as you say, and 'twill be well with me," she murmured.

Her mother took the seat opposite them and sighed. "I would rather see her betrothed to Madame Luchaire's prized swine." All three laughed.

" 'Tis true enough there is not much difference in girth or smell," Jeanine said.

"I am sorry, daughter. It seems the only way. Had the trade been better, had the ships not run aground, I might have kept you for our house alone. But there must always come a day of settling accounts. Our Lord God makes that clear. To everyone there comes a season of reckoning. Colbert holds the power to see us all put to debtors' prison and left to rot."

"I understand." And in truth, Jeanine did comprehend the gravity of the situation. The entire town joined together could not have understood her plight any better.

"I have but one request," her father said, reaching out to take her hand. "One prayer."

"What is it?" she asked, looking first to her mother as if to gain the truth in her eyes.

Her mother reached out a hand to lightly touch Jeanine's free hand.

"I ask that you might forgive me," her father said softly. " 'Twas not my desire to come to this end. My own mismanagement and lack of foresight has brought us to this ruin. I ask your forgiveness for bartering you into marriage with Antoine Colbert."

"Forgive me, too." Her mother's eyes were filled with tears. "For we know the kind of man he is, and your father did not accept this arrangement lightly."

Jeanine saw the anguish in their expressions and knelt beside the table to humble herself before them. "I know 'twas not your wish to marry me to Monsieur Colbert. There is nothing to forgive. You had no other choice. The trade is poor, and my brother is long overdue from the sea. You have more worries than my marriage. Rest assured that I will trust God for my existence."

Evening vespers were managed in a spirit of heaviness. Papa prayed for the safe return of his son, Étienne, whose ship the *Crispin* was long overdue. He prayed, too, that God might in some way save his daughter from marriage to Antoine Colbert, and if not, that God might transform Colbert into a man of Christian honor.

Jeanine listened as her father prayed on behalf of each member of his family. She wanted so much to have faith that God would deliver her from this nightmare. She wanted to know peace for her future and to feel hope once again that all would be well. It was true that she was twenty years old and that most women her age were already married and had children. Ofttimes they were widowed. But she had remained in her father's house, quietly keeping faith with her parents, carding and weaving wool, helping in whatever manner her mother desired. She had known real happiness in her life with them, and now she could see that joy slipping away.

Lifting her head while her father continued to pray, Jeanine felt an ache in her heart at the thought of leaving them. Her mother was so fragile, and she longed to remain at her side to continue aiding her. Her well-trained eye told her that Margarite de la Fontaine might not have many more years of health, mayhap even life, and Jeanine longed to keep company with her beloved mother for as long as possible.

Then, too, her father held the very core of her heart. She had been the doted-upon daughter, the youngest child who held favor in her father's eye. Never had he returned from his trade trips abroad, but what he had brought her some special trinket. She knew full well that she held his heart in her hand. If only she could prevent the deeds that were soon to be upon them.

Having concluded their prayers, Jeanine received her parents' blessing and slipped upstairs to the third floor where her bedroom allowed her the most privacy of any place in the house. Fear gripped her heart, and she longed for someone to shake her awake and declare it all nothing more than a bad dream. Moonlight filtered into her room through the pasty thick glass of her window, drawing her—beckoning her to come stand in the glow. It was impossible to make clear the images outside through the thick glass, but somewhere out there Antoine Colbert was planning her future.

"Why, Father?" she whispered reverently. "Why must this happen? Why must I suffer this fate?"

two

As the weeks slipped by, Jeanine became more despondent. She tried to keep busy in order not to dwell upon the inevitability of her marriage, but more often than not, despair was her most obvious companion.

Needing to escape the reminders of her future with Colbert, Jeanine took herself from the house and made her way down the cobblestone road. Her one thought was to seek solace at her grandmother's grave. *Grandmère* de la Fontaine had died some four years earlier, but the memory of their closeness lived on in Jeanine's heart. Bundling up against the harsh winter cold, Jeanine made her way to the small cemetery where her grandmother had been laid to rest.

The wind whipped mercilessly at her clothes, and casting a quick glance at the skies overhead, Jeanine feared the imminent arrival of yet another storm. Pulling her thin cloak tighter, Jeanine knelt beside the grave and let out a heavy sigh. Her warm breath puffed out against the frigid air, and with it, Jeanine felt her hopes slip away as well.

"I tried hard to be brave, *Grandmère*," she whispered to the gravestone. " 'Tis not my desire to give my parents reason to be overburdened with grief, but you know how difficult this is for me. To marry that pig, Colbert," she said, from behind clenched teeth, "makes me want to retch."

For all her short years, Jeanine had seen a great many reasons to find marriage to one such as Colbert a dismal prospect. Colbert was a wealthy landowner with a great many properties and investments. He was a staunch supporter of the French king, Charles VI, while most of Bruges, in fact most of Flanders, aligned itself with the English king, Richard II. The situation had been in dispute since William the Conqueror had taken England in 1066, and still the two countries made war over the issue. At last, however, they were enjoying a sort of peace. A de facto truce had begun in 1380 and had somehow managed to linger—mostly because the English were still arguing over Richard's position on the throne. He'd been barely nine years old when King Edward III had died in 1377 and had just reached his majority the year before, in 1389.

There remained in the country an air of constant upheaval because of the torn loyalties. Flanders remained, overall, a supporter of English rule, but because it was only a small province, it appeared futile to hope that it might have the rest of France see things its way.

"Oh, *Grandmère,* it all seems so hopeless." Jeanine sighed and muttered a phrase she had heard since a child whenever calamity struck: *"Dieu m'a fait compagnon à Job."* God has made me a companion for Job.

Indeed, that was what Jeanine felt like. Job of the Bible had found himself tested sorely. He had lost most all that he loved and cared about, coming close to the point of death, but only enough to share in the miseries of life. She thought of Latin Scriptures read in the great cathedral and those shared to her in a more common French by her dear friend Doctor Grosz.

Job had sat in the midst of his miseries, lamenting, "What is my strength, that I should hope?"

Jeanine wondered the same. "How can I have hope amid this nightmare?" She looked heavenward. Her conversation with the stone and her grandmother's memory concluded. *"Mon Dieu,* where is my hope?" Her prayerful question brought little but turmoil to her heart. Her hope should be in God, Himself. But she felt as though He might well have closed a door between them when Antoine Colbert stepped into the room. Perhaps God had arranged a test of faith for her, just as He had allowed Satan to test the faithfulness of Job.

"Please, Lord God, do not test me as Job," Jeanine prayed. "I am not of his strength, and my faith is most weak. You know my heart. It is not my desire that any portion of it might belong to anyone save You. Please hear my cry and deliver me from the hands of mine enemy—Antoine Colbert."

She had barely breathed the prayer when a tiny voice called to her. "Mademoiselle Jeanine."

Getting to her feet, Jeanine immediately recognized a small boy. "Jacques, what are you about that you should trudge through the cold to be at my side?"

"I have a message for you. 'Tis from Dr. Grosz."

Jeanine nodded and took the small slip of paper. *"Merci beaucoup!"* The boy nodded in acknowledgment of her thanks and hurried back toward the heart of town.

Jeanine unfolded the paper and read the simple words. "Five geese flying." It was their agreed message should Dr. Grosz required Jeanine's assistance. Refolding the paper, she put it into the pocket of her apron and hurried back to her father's house.

For several years, Jeanine had been making her excuses and taking leave of her mother to perform a most unusual service for the poor and destitute. With the help of her aged friend Dr. Grosz, Jeanine had found a passion for medicine and the art of surgery. But such things were clearly illegal for women to participate in. It seemed only fitting, however, that because Dr. Grosz was Jewish and therefore also forbidden to practice medicine in Bruges, the two should conspire to create their own hospital of sorts.

Simon Grosz lived near the docks on the River Zwin, and because his home was really no more than a hovel, he was fairly ignored by those in powerful positions. But Simon meant the world to Jeanine and to the poor, who gladly kept his secret. Jeanine had met him one day walking back from seeing her father's ship off. Her father had planned a northerly route by sea to the harbor of Danzig, and because he would be gone for such a long time, Jeanine had donned her brother Étienne's heavy, more masculine cloak and dared a venture to the docks.

No one had bothered her, and even her father had been startled to find his comely daughter behind the protective covering of her brother's cloak. He had taken her to the privacy of his cabin, chided her sternly for such foolishness, then kissed her soundly and embraced her with much love. She was his favorite, and well she knew it. But it had given her much cause for reflection on her attitude and actions.

"Poor Father," she thought, making her way along the same cobblestone roadway that had taken her to the docks so many years ago. "It isn't his fault that the river is filling with silt. He's a good businessman, but now he will have to find flat-bottomed boats or make his trade routes over land."

Simon's residence loomed up ahead. It looked like any one of a number of ramshackle riverfront buildings. Two stories in total, it was joined on either side by two other places of business. Outside the building, each of the businesses hung rickety signs that announced their professions. Simon's sign was a book, and it was well-known to all that he was a copier of written work. But among the poor and poverty-stricken souls who lived and worked along the docks, it was just as well-known that the old man was a physician of extraordinary ability.

Jeanine never failed to marvel at how the people protected their dear Dr. Grosz. It was hard to maintain a prejudice against a man who had just saved your child from disease or reset the broken leg of a man who by another physician would have seen it cut away and cauterized in order to be done with it. In spite of their superstitions and fears of religious excommunication, the people kept Dr. Grosz's secret, and hers as well.

Jeanine nodded to a passerby and smiled against the wintry cold as she pushed open the thin wooden door to Simon Grosz's shop. Inside, the front room bore all the signs of being a legitimate copy shop. The copy table stood against the wall where the room's single window allowed light to flood across the writing board. Beside the board a sheet of parchment awaited the quill. There were assorted tools—a razor for scraping, a pumice stone, a narrow ruler for accurate lining of the text, and a boar's tooth for polishing. Jeanine knew that in the drawer of the table there would be quills and ink. Everything necessary to copy a book.

"Bonjour! Bonjour!" Simon greeted her enthusiastically. "I was afraid Jacques would not find you. Twice he returned to me saying, 'She is not at home.' So I think to myself, 'Where could she be on such a day?' "

Jeanine laughed and removed her cloak. "And you knew I would be visiting my *grandmère's* grave, *non?*"

"But of course," Simon said, taking her cloak to hang it by the door. "Come. We have a great deal of work to do. I have a young boy who has a fishing hook imbedded near his eye. My own eyes are too blind for such close work, and I knew that you would be just the one to assist me. The boy will not be so frightened when he learns of your gentle touch."

Jeanine nodded and immediately began to unfasten the

elaborately embroidered belt which snugly encircled her waist. The very simple lines of her houppeland made it easy to change into her disguise. The gown was utilized by both men and women and hung as a shapeless shift to the floor and boasted overly long, full sleeves. Both men and women wore houppelands, the only difference being the manner in which they were belted or decorated. Men sometimes didn't bother to gird the flowing robe with a belt, but women generally did. It provided the perfect way to decorate and brighten their gown and to show off their tiny waists.

Jeanine slipped into the back room to change her very feminine houppeland of pale blue and lavender for a more masculine one of black. She didn't belt the robe, but left the gown to hang, hiding her very feminine figure from view. Her long curly brown hair was tightly braided up and secured under a man's woolen head cap. Simon had ingeniously sewn some of his own course hair along the bottom ridge of the cap, giving Jeanine an even more masculine appearance. She then took mud and ashes and smeared her face and neck until they were amply darkened. This too added to her appearing more masculine, and she checked her reflection in the mirror before joining Simon.

"Ah, Doctor Font," he said with a smile. " 'Tis good to have you join me. I have great work for you today."

Jeanine smiled and gave a deep-throated, "By your leave, *Monsieur Docteur*."

It was only when she was operating as a physician that Jeanine felt truly whole. She had long believed that God had called her to heal people, but the law was clearly against women participating in the healing arts as licensed physicians. Much more, Jeanine enjoyed surgical procedures, which by the admission of even the most knowledgeable man, were in their infancy and scarcely understood. Even the church had come out against surgery as being spiritually depraved. But Jeanine found that when she could help a dying person recover, she had actually allowed herself to be used of God. When she helped to deliver a newborn, she felt the thrill of life in her hands and the glory of God's wondrous power. How could that be wrong?

Of course the lies she found necessary to tell her parents and others were very wrong. She had lived with the weight of such deceit for so long that she hadn't even realized the heavy burden it had become. Jeanine knew it would have been impossible to explain her missions to her parents. They would have feared for her well-being. Having a young maiden in the area of the docks was worry enough, without that young woman performing an illegal act. But the poor people needed her, and it seemed that her lies were justifiable. Surely God understood.

Simon had already seen to cleansing the boy's wounds and also to giving him an herbal balm of mandrake to induce sleep. The boy now slept in perfect silence, unmindful of the procedure that lay ahead. Jeanine took up her instruments and worked cautiously over the small boy for over an hour. She found the fishing hook a great challenge to master. If it had entered an inch to the left, it would have embedded itself deep into the boy's eye. The barbs made it impossible to pull back through the opening. They would catch and embed themselves deeper into the flesh should they be pulled upon. With gentle care, Jeanine finally managed to direct the hook upward. It created yet another wound of exit, but it did far less damage to the tissue beneath the surface of his skin. Blood trickled from the hole, and Jeanine immediately set to cleansing the wound with egg whites, a common help for purification.

The boy's mother watched with horror as the procedure concluded when Jeanine secured a bandage at the side of her son's eye. Wearily, Jeanine straightened up and met the mother's expression.

"He'll be as good as new," Jeanine said with a low gravelly voice. "You must leave the bandage in place, however, and return to me in three days' time."

"Oh, *Docteur*," the mother said, openly weeping. "It was all my fault. I should never have let him go to the boat with his father. He's too young to be left unattended."

Jeanine smiled sympathetically and patted the woman on the back as she had observed Simon do on many occasions. "Do not fret. The Blessed Father has looked over you this day. Your son will heal. Setting blame will not retrace your steps, nor will it speed his recovery."

The teary-eyed woman nodded. "We are very poor. I have no money with which to pay, but if you have no wife, perhaps I could offer my services to clean or cook. I am a good cook."

"*Non,*" replied Jeanine. "I do my service unto the Lord. He will provide the pay as well."

"Oh, *merci! Merci!*" She fell to her knees and kissed Jeanine's cloak. The woman was incredibly dirty, and as her tears fell, they caused streaks against her dirt-laden face. "May God bless and keep you all your days," she managed to say.

Jeanine touched her head. "And may He keep you and your family as well."

Jeanine went to wash her hands as Simon helped the woman to collect her sleeping child. There was a deep sense of satisfaction in having given of herself, and to Jeanine, it mattered very little that she couldn't preform her feats of medicinal wonder for all the world to see. She had meant what she'd said. She was working unto the Lord God in heaven. He knew her hands and their work. He had blessed her in ways that she did not yet begin to understand.

"If only You would tell me of this marriage to Antoine Colbert," she whispered, glancing upward. "If only You would show me a means of escape."

"So you have made yet another conquest, Dr. Font," Simon said, entering the room as Jeanine toweled her hands.

"He was so sweet. Did you see his precious little face? He will not suffer overmuch with his new scar. Mayhap it will give the ladies something to fancy when he grows into a fine young man, eh?"

Simon laughed and took a seat behind a sturdy desk. He pulled out several copies of well-worn medical books and motioned Jeanine to take a seat. "I have received an addition to these books," he said conspiratorially. "People think it not odd for a book copier to have medical works. Good thing they do not know I am rapidly going blind and would find copy work quite impossible. But if my eyes would but allow, I would copy this book over many times."

Jeanine nodded. "What new book do you speak of?"

Simon beamed a brilliant smile. "A copy of Mondino de' Luzzi's book of anatomy entitled, *Anthania*."

Jeanine nearly squealed with delight as she reached out to take the book in hand. She opened it and skimmed the pages. "It's in French!" she declared, quite delighted, for most medical books were in Latin and difficult for her to read. "Oh, Simon, it's marvelous. What a find."

"Oui," Simon replied. "I thought you might find pleasure in this."

" 'After the muscle, the bones. Now the bones of the chest are many and are not continuous,' " she read from the text. "This is truly wonderful. Just imagine what I can learn from this." Thoughts danced madly in her head.

"Which is precisely why I intend to send it home with you this very day. I have secured for you a false-bottomed basket. That way, should anyone stop you and search your wares, they will find nothing but the simple treasures of a maiden."

Jeanine grinned. "This is a blessing from God."

"What a difference time makes." Simon's face seemed to reflect a memory of something long gone.

"How so?"

The old man gently rubbed his coarse gray beard. "I was thinking back to my time at the university in Montpellier. It was the only university to allow a Jew to study medicine. I was—"

"Docteur! Docteur!" a deep male voice called from the alleyway door.

Jeanine immediately got to her feet and handed the book back to Simon. "I will see what the commotion is about."

She went quickly to the door and opened it to find a trusted friend. "Pierre, what is wrong?" she asked the burly sailor.

"There is a ship come just now to harbor. There are several injured on board, but one man in particular lies close to death."

Jeanine felt her stomach lurch. Her father's ship, the *Crispin*, was long overdue, and Étienne de la Fontaine, her brother, was the ship's captain. "Which ship was it, Pierre?"

"The *Crispin*," he replied, confirming her suspicions.

"Tell them the doctor will be there posthaste." Pierre nodded and was gone, while Jeanine turned back to face Simon. Great turmoil churned in her heart. " 'Tis my father's ship, and my brother sailed her. If I go to the docks there is a chance they will recognize me."

"But if you do not go, good men may die. Your brother included."

"Oui," Jeanine replied with a heavy sigh. "I will go, and you must pray for me."

"But my friend, I pray always for you," Simon replied.

❧

The commotion surrounding the *Crispin* left Jeanine with a churning sense of fear. Was her brother alive? Was he one of the injured? She moved quickly, trying to take long masculine strides and praying all the time that no one would recognize her as a woman.

"Make way! Make way!" Pierre called when he spotted Dr. Font in the gathering crowd.

The injured men were being moved from the ship and brought down the gangplank as Jeanine approached. She searched each face, feeling both relief that her brother didn't occupy one of the litters and compassion for each man's miseries.

"This man's arm is broken," she growled out and then checked the head wound he'd received. "He's not mortally wounded," she announced, feeling that the skull was firm. She quickly moved on.

The next man suffered a crushed left leg and would most likely require an amputation. The man after that was already dead.

"What happened?" she asked, as a sailor halted in front of her.

"A storm," the man replied as if further explanation was unnecessary.

"A storm?" she questioned.

"*Oui.* The main mast snapped in two. Three men were swept out to sea amid the waves."

"Where is your captain?" she asked, almost forgetting to lower her voice. She felt desperate to see Étienne. To know that he was well.

"On board. He was unharmed, but he tends the most critically injured man."

She breathed a sigh of relief. Étienne lived! Pushing her way on board, Jeanine came upon her brother and would have flung herself into his arms had her identity not been disguised. He looked weary from his ordeal. Several small cuts and bruises marred his handsome face, but other than that he appeared well.

"Are you injured?"

"Non," he replied. "But this good fellow has suffered mightily." Étienne clearly wanted the focus moved from his own needs.

Jeanine forced herself to look away from her brother. The ashen, unconscious face of the man on the litter, struck her deeply. He was handsome and carried the look of a nobleman, but his temple revealed an ugly bruising that instantly worried Jeanine. Gently she ran her fingers along the lines of his skull. The indentation was obvious when her hand pressed against the temple. "The skull is fractured. He will have to be taken to a place where I might care for him. Come. I will lead the way."

"His name is Victor Pindar," Étienne offered. "He is an Englishman."

Jeanine tried to maintain her masculine attitude. " 'Tis sure he will be a dead man if we do not see him rapidly taken from this ship."

Étienne motioned Pierre and another stocky worker to grab up the litter. "Follow this good doctor. He will instruct you." The men nodded and Jeanine breathed a sigh of relief. Étienne had not recognized her.

Back at Simon's, Jeanine worked feverishly over Victor. His body had sustained multiple injuries, including several broken ribs and two rather nasty gashes along his right thigh. Simon had his own hands busy with the other patients, and no one seemed to question whether he had a right to practice medicine. The dockworkers knew the old man and his young assistant, Dr. Font, and little else mattered. The poor had an inner-working of communication, and word of mouth was quick to spread that Dr. Font and Dr. Grosz could be trusted. It was also understood that for reasons both known and unknown, the doctors were not allowed to practice medicine under the scrutiny of the public eye. Therefore, they were quite cautious about letting anyone know about their good doctors.

Jeanine bathed Victor's head wound, far and away the most serious of his injuries. The discoloration was spreading, and the man refused to regain consciousness, making it quite evident that the brain was hemorrhaging. If she didn't do something quickly, Victor Pindar would die.

"Simon," she whispered. The old man glanced up from where he was stitching the wounds of another man. "This will take us both," she added.

Simon finished his work and came to stand beside her. "He's nearly dead," he said in a tone that suggested she give him over to God.

"*Oui,* but I think we still might save him."

"The pressure from the blood must be relieved or he will die," Simon said, palpating the depressed temple.

Jeanine knew for herself that too much time was slipping by "Can we drill into it? Will not the blood then come through the opening and relieve his brain of the pressure? You have oft' told me of trephining. Might we try it now?"

"Yes, but it isn't a simple procedure. It is most dangerous, and it could prove to be his death."

Jeanine shook her head. "But this will prove to be his death if we do not at least attempt it."

Simon nodded and went to retrieve his instruments. While he was busily preparing for the dangerous surgery, Jeanine found her hand brushing back the brownish black hair of her patient. She felt a tenderness for the man that she could not explain. Her heart ached with the sight of him damaged and wounded from the storm. She tried to imagine him healthy and vital as he must have been before the accident.

"Dear God, help us to heal this man," Jeanine whispered. What was his name? Étienne had told her, but for some reason it had slipped her mind. Victor, something. Yes, that was it. Victor Pindar. She continued to stroke his hair as though in doing so she might somehow induce him to live.

"Here we are," Simon said, laying out the instruments they would need. "Call Pierre to help, just in case the man wakes up."

Jeanine nodded and went into the alleyway where Pierre was giving water to several of the less critically injured men. "Pierre," she called, "we are going to preform a serious surgery and need your assistance."

The burly man nodded and handed the water bucket to one of his companions. Jeanine led him to the washstand where she thoroughly scrubbed her hands and then motioned Pierre to follow suit.

"First," Simon said, "we must clear away the hair. My eyes are not so good, Dr. Font. You will have to be responsible for this surgery, but I will guide you as you perform."

"Me?" Jeanine found herself squeaking out the word. "You want me to. . ." She couldn't say the words.

"You will do fine. Remember, this is what you have spent so many hours in study for."

"But I've not yet studied this type of surgery," she protested.

"Then you are about to," Simon said with a smile of reassurance.

Carefully they considered the wound and decided how best to continue. They pulled back the thick hair and shaved clean a portion of scalp. This done, Jeanine cut into the soft flesh, and while Simon held back the patch of skin, she took up yet another instrument to saw into the bone of Victor's skull. Carefully, with Simon's constant instruction, she maneuvered artfully until the tiny circle of bone was removed and dark blood began to seep out.

"We will allow the blood to drain, and as it does, our patient may well become conscious. We will have to be careful that he not thrash about."

Jeanine nodded, grateful that Simon and Pierre had already tied Victor securely to the table. Pierre stood alert at the man's side, prepared to restrain the man if necessary.

When Victor showed signs of movement, Simon felt that enough blood had been drained in order to complete their surgery. Together, he and Jeanine worked until only the raw, freshly stitched patch remained to show their work. With any luck, the thickness of his hair would hide the scar.

Victor's moans began before Jeanine had secured the last stitch, but it wasn't until some minutes later that he actually opened his eyes.

"Eleanor." He moaned the name over and over.

"Perhaps his wife," Simon suggested.

Jeanine nodded, feeling sudden disappointment. Of course the man was probably married. He looked to be ten years her senior. He probably had a fine wife and a great many children who were even now wondering where their father might be.

But she didn't want there to be a wife and children. For reasons that she couldn't understand or comprehend, Jeanine wanted Victor Pindar for herself.

Shaking her head at such a ridiculous thought, Jeanine tried to busy herself by collecting the instruments. Why should she think such a thing? She had only just laid eyes on him. There was no telling who he was, or what kind of man he had been. Beyond that, Jeanine was in no way available to consider such matters. She was betrothed to another man, a man whose happiness meant settled debts and peace of mind for her father.

With a sad resignation that made her feel aged, Jeanine pushed aside the image of the handsome face and his murmurings for a woman who didn't even know he lay perilously close to death.

three

For several days, Jeanine managed to sneak away from her mother's watchful eyes and make her way to Simon's. It was becoming increasingly difficult, however, to come up with a good excuse for her absences, and Jeanine knew it would not be long before she would be hard-pressed to leave for any reason.

Lies mounted on top of lies, and Jeanine felt great sorrow in her deeds. Her mother would be sorely wounded at learning of her daughter's deception, yet even this could not make Jeanine give up her plan. The only real problem was her impending marriage to Antoine Colbert. No matter how Jeanine prayed that her heavenly Father might give her direction and take the responsibility from her, God seemed silent on why she should suffer such a fate.

Securing her disguise in place once again, Jeanine emerged from Simon's back room as Dr. Font. Putting thoughts of her betrothal aside, she hurried to learn the news of her patient. She longed to see Victor and know of his night under Simon's care. Each day seemed to bring only welcomed news. He was much improved—this much she had ascertained for herself in previous days. Nevertheless, she longed to see him. To know that he was healing and that he would recover without any permanent damage.

"*Bonjour,* Simon," she said in a low husky voice.

"Ah, I knew you would come with the first crowing of the cock," Simon answered with a smile. "I did not hear you come in. I was with our patient."

"How is he?" she asked in a whisper, her gaze darting to the room which housed Victor Pindar.

"He is recovering well. I changed the dressings on his leg wounds and found them healing nicely. His ribs will be bound yet for another week before we test them to see how they are faring."

"And his head?"

"Much improved," Simon answered, preparing to mix a concoction of herbs together. "Why don't you see for yourself?"

Jeanine nodded and slipped quietly into Victor's room.

"You are the doctor, are you not?" the man's voice called weakly to her in English.

Jeanine didn't understand the words very well, but *doctor* sounded close enough to *docteur,* that she felt confident of his meaning.

"I am *Docteur* Font," she said in slowly spoken French. "Do you speak my language?" She came to his bedside and caught sight of his weathered face. His dark eyes beheld her for a moment before closing.

"Oui," he managed behind a grimace of pain.

"You are in pain?" she said, barely remembering to keep her voice low.

"Oui."

"Your head?" she questioned, checking the incision for signs of infection. "You have sustained a bad wound. The mast of my. . ." She paused. She'd nearly said, *The mast of my brother's ship.* That would never do. She pretended to examine his head first one way and then another, all the while trying to calm her raging heart. "The mast broke and fell upon you. Your skull sustained a heavy blow."

"I don't remember what happened," he said softly.

Jeanine was momentarily mesmerized as he licked his dry, chapped lips. "No, I supposed you might not. 'Tis not unusual. Injuries to the brain are difficult to understand. We do not yet know what makes one man completely lose his senses and another regain his memories when consciousness is lost. There are theories, of course, but that is unimportant to you, *non?*"

"It is important to me to get a message to England."

Jeanine was once again reminded of the name Eleanor and the possibility that this man belonged to another woman. "A message?" she managed to question gruffly.

"*Oui.* My sister, Eleanor, resides in Dover with her young son, Marcus. I live there, and I am long overdue. She will be heartsick."

Jeanine let out a long-held breath. Eleanor was his sister. He had no wife. Or did he? "And what of your wife?" she questioned. "Your children? Should we not also send a message to them?"

"There is no wife. No children."

Just then Simon returned with a glass. "I have prepared a potion which will give you relief from your sufferings and aid healing."

"What have you prepared?" Jeanine asked.

"Sweet marjoram to help heal the brain," Simon answered, handing Victor the glass. "Fruit of the mandragora to induce sleep and dull the senses of pain, and fennel to control brain fever."

Jeanine's eyes widened as Victor drank down the smelly brew. "Has he suffered brain fever?"

Simon smiled. "*Non.* 'Tis certain the fennel is working, eh?"

Jeanine nodded and followed Simon reluctantly from the room. "Will he sleep right away?" she asked, keeping her voice to a bare whisper.

"The medicine is potent. It should work quickly. Why do you ask?"

Jeanine glanced at the still-open door. "He mentioned a sister in England. One to whom a message should be delivered."

"Eleanor?"

Jeanine nodded. "The same. He lives with her in Dover. There is no wife or children, and besides this sister 'tis my thought that he is alone."

" 'Twould seem amiss for us to delay in sending the message," Simon said, eyeing her strangely.

Jeanine felt her face grow hot and was grateful for once to be smeared in ashes and mud. "I just thought to obtain the place where the message should be sent. Surely Dover is so large a town that we would need a more specific address."

Simon smiled and nodded. "Go back to him then. Sit for a time if it brings you comfort." He seemed to understand her longing without Jeanine having to confess her feelings.

" 'Twould seem fitting," she replied and quickly took herself to Victor's bedside before Simon could take back his words.

Victor appeared to hear her enter, for when she approached his bedside, he opened his eyes and looked up in anticipation of what she might next do.

"You did not tell me where I might send word to your sister," she said in a strained, masculine tone.

Victor seemed to consider this for a moment before yawning and closing his eyes. "She is on her estate. The lands belonging once to her dead husband, Lord Bramston."

Jeanine memorized the name and adjusted the pillow on which Victor's head rested somewhat more easily. "Is the draught helping with the pain?"

"I. . .believe 'tis. . .better. . .now." His voice was weak. The medicine was helping him off to sleep.

Jeanine pulled up a chair and sat by the bedside. "I will wait here to make certain you fall asleep," she murmured. "And I will offer up a blessing for you as well." She thought for a moment, then continued. "May the Lord God heal you now. May He see your needs and reach where human hands may not go."

Victor seemed not to hear. For a moment he appeared peaceful, then he reached out to touch her hand. "There is trouble with the buttresses," he whispered. "You must see to them." He turned toward her as if to sit up, winced in pain, and fell back against the mattress, even as Jeanine put a hand to his shoulder to still him. "The cathedral. . . must finish." He moaned. "Transepts. . .uneven."

Jeanine stared at him in wonder. What manner of thing did he speak of? Buttresses and transepts? She leaned closer to better hear him, but just as she did he lapsed into English, and further understanding was completely lost to her. He muttered softly for several minutes before finally settling into a deep sleep. With a sigh, Jeanine touched his brow and a longing grew within her to better know his face—his hands.

Tenderly, she picked up his hand from where it had fallen away from her own. His hands were large, with long slender fingers that appeared well-groomed and cared for. She longed to ask her brother about him, but it escaped her how she might bring up the subject. Étienne had spent most of his time assessing the ship's damage, as had her father. When the men had returned at close of day, they were exhausted and surly, completely unwilling to discuss much of anything. Beyond that, for all they knew, Jeanine had never met Victor Pindar. And because his recuperation was spent at Simon's and not in her home, Jeanine might never have reason to express her concern or interest.

After leaving Victor's side to study with Simon, Jeanine felt restlessness overcome her. Her mind refused to remain on her studies, and in spite of the fact that Simon continued in his patient manner, Jeanine could no longer deal with the issues of anatomy.

"I wish I did not have to leave him here," she said, staring longingly at the closed door for the tenth or eleventh time. Then worried that Simon might misunderstand her reasoning, she added, " 'Tis naught to do with your good work, however."

Simon closed his book and leaned back in the chair. "Dr. Font is worried about his patient, eh? Or is it Mademoiselle Jeanine has lost her heart, and Monsieur Pindar holds the secrets to where we might reclaim it."

Jeanine blushed. "I suppose I am being but a twiddle-headed girl. Truly 'tis not what I planned." She sighed and looked Simon in the eye. "He makes me feel. . .well. . .I don't really have words for how I feel."

"Perhaps you are sick," Simon suggested teasingly.

"Heartsick, mayhap." She got up and shook her head. "Medicine has become my life. I have no interest in marrying Antoine Colbert, even though our wedding is but a short time away. 'Twould suit me better to join a nunnery, but then again 'twould be impossible to practice surgery there."

Simon laughed. "As though 'twould not be the same with Monsieur Colbert." Jeanine frowned. "Forgive me, Jeanine, I did not mean—"

" 'Tis all right. You speak but the truth. How might I fault you for that, dear friend? You are right. 'Twill be most impossible to slip away from Antoine and come here. I will find myself forced to tend only those around me, and surely there will be no practicing of surgery."

The cathedral bells chimed out the hour, causing Jeanine

to start. "Oh, my! 'Tis noon already. I must hurry home."
She began pulling off her cap. "I will check back later this
day if I find a proper excuse for leaving the house."

"Never fear, my dear *docteur,* I will see to our patient's
care. Should I need you—should he worsen, I will send
someone for you."

❧

That night over dinner, Jeanine was pleasantly surprised to
find her brother and father in residence. The hour was early
and their spirits were light, which led Jeanine to believe
that things were going well with the ship's recovery.

"Another day, maybe two," her father announced, "and
we should see the completion of the repairs."

" 'Tis good news indeed," her mother said with a smile.

They ate in silence for several minutes, before Jeanine
dared ask the question on her mind. "And how is your
friend, Étienne?"

Her brother stared dumbly at her for a moment, then
smiled. "Oh, you're speaking of Monsieur Pindar, *non?*"

"Yes," she smiled. "I believe that was his name. Is he
well now?"

"To tell you the truth," her brother replied, "I haven't
had time to check in on him. I turned him over to the
capable hands of a doctor, and that was the last of it. He
isn't actually a friend, you know. He simply was a man in
need of passage home. I told him I could bring him to
Calais, but after that he would have to find passage to
England. Of course, the storm put an end to that."

" 'Tis a pity he must suffer without the care of those
who love him," Jeanine replied, trying hard to concentrate
on her bread and cheese.

To her surprise and relief, her mother took up the conversation. "I quite agree. 'Tis unseemly for you to leave
him with strangers. I cannot say that I know what you

were thinking when you performed this most uncharitable act."

Étienne seemed genuinely wounded. "I had only the desire to see him put into the care of a doctor. 'Tis my own fault that I've not taken up his cause beyond that."

"You could find Monsieur Pindar," Jeanine encouraged. "Perhaps if he is still ill, he could recuperate here. I would gladly give up my room to help such a man."

Étienne laughed. "No doubt your Monsieur Colbert would bring down this house with his rage if he were to learn that you had taken another man into your room."

Jeanine gasped. "What scandal do you speak? I only meant to imply that I would be happy to help in caring for the man. After all, 'twould be our Christian duty. Would it not?"

"I think Jeanine has a point," her mother replied. "The man is a stranger in our land. He was injured aboard our boat. Now let us do an act of charity and care for him while he recovers. Surely 'twould be fitting."

"I hadn't considered it," Jeanine's father inserted before his son could answer, "but such plans seem quite reasonable. Étienne, why not go fetch the man home this very night?"

"I promise I will," Étienne replied.

Jeanine smiled to herself in satisfaction. Tonight, with providence and God on their side, Victor Pindar would be a patient in her house. Not only her house, her very room! Suddenly things seemed quite different. Here, in her own home, Jeanine could be a woman and care for him as a woman. At Simon's she had found it necessary to maintain her disguise and remain a man. There was no hope of sharing her interest in him if he couldn't even spend time during his recovery to see her as a woman.

"When will you go after him?" Jeanine asked, trying

hard not to sound overly interested.

Étienne looked at the expectant faces of his parents and sibling. Grabbing up a piece of bread, he stood. "I suppose I might just as well go now. 'Tis of a certainty I will be without any peace 'til I do.

Jeanine too jumped to her feet. "I'll go prepare the room now." She smiled to herself and hummed all the way up the stairs. Victor Pindar was going to be her private patient, and because she would help to heal him in her own home, no one would accuse her falsely for dabbling in medical procedures.

four

"Here are clean linens," Jeanine's mother said, entering the bedroom and placing the stack on a nearby stool.

"I have stripped off the old linens and turned the mattress. 'Tis certain that it would be more comfortable with another stuffing of feathers, but 'twill have to do for now," Jeanine said, staring blankly at the mattress. In her mind's eye she was envisioning Victor in sleep upon her bed. Dreamily, she reached down to smooth out the mattress, then quickly pulled back her hand, suddenly realizing how foolish she might appear to her mother.

Her mother seemed not to notice, however. She was busying herself by taking up the two modest rugs. "I'll take these for a good pounding," she said.

Jeanine nodded and hurried to remake the bed, anxious to have her room in order. After this task was complete, she rushed around to insure that the remaining portions of the room were fit as well. Her small dressing table, cluttered with a variety of herbs and healing balms, as well as various other trinkets, nearly cried for her attention, but Jeanine couldn't take the time to put things in order. Already she heard voices in the main room below, and her heart pounded faster. Could they have already returned?

Hurrying, she unbound her hair and combed through the thick brown ringlets. All of her life she had wanted to curse the curls that naturally formed on her head. Most of the time she wore her hair braided and hidden from view, but she wanted to look feminine and pretty, something she seldom cared about. Running the brush through the waist-long mane, Jeanine smiled to herself. Tonight, Victor would see her for the first time as a woman. Perhaps then, he, too, would lose his heart. One final smoothing of the curls, and Jeanine replaced the brush and went in search of her brother and Victor.

The home of François de la Fontaine was a relatively simple four-story structure. The first floor was devoted to his merchandise and business affairs. The second floor was the main floor for the family. It was here that they dined and shared quiet times in front of the fire. The third floor was devoted to bedrooms, while the upper level contained the overflow of the other three floors.

Jeanine made her way down the stairs, struggling to keep her heart from pounding right through her chest. She felt like a giddy schoolgirl and knew it was silly. She chided herself to calm down, but never having ever felt this way about any man, she was almost relieved to experience the feelings. She had despaired of ever falling in love, and now she was certain that with little or no effort, she could be deeply in love with Victor Pindar.

Reaching the final step, Jeanine felt light as a feather and nearly danced across the room to find her family. What she found instead was Antoine Colbert.

"My, my," he said, low and seductively, "but you are bewitching."

Jeanine froze in place. The smile faded from her countenance. "What are you doing here?" she asked.

"I came to see you," he replied and stepped forward.

Jeanine caught a whiff of his stench and grimaced. "My father has not yet returned, but when he does you may keep your company with him."

"Why would I desire to keep his company, when I have a beautiful wife to consider."

"I am not yet your wife, monsieur," she replied defiantly.

Her chin lifted ever so slightly in the air as Colbert frowned.

" 'Tis yet another reason I am come. What say we put an end to the final three weeks of waiting. I would see our marriage take place on the morrow."

"Impossible!" Jeanine exclaimed, feeling sudden revulsion at the thought of Colbert's wishes being adhered to. "My father is even now retrieving a very ill comrade into our home. I will be needed to assist my mother in his care. There is no possible time to plan a wedding at this point. Mayhap," she said, pausing thoughtfully, "we might delay it another fortnight beyond."

"Never," Colbert said, crossing the distance between them. Without warning his pudgy fingers closed over her hands. "You are mine, mademoiselle, and I will have what I want." He pulled her closer, but Jeanine pushed at him, backing away.

"I do not love you, monsieur. Surely 'twould be a better marriage to seek a woman whose heart is not set against you."

"I care not where your heart is set," he said. Again he stepped forward, only this time he backed Jeanine against a wall. Letting go of her hands, he gripped her arms tightly. They were nearly the same height, so their gazes met equally as they stood only inches apart. Colbert's thick stomach aided his hands in holding Jeanine in place, and she fought to push him away, sickened at the thought of his touch. Colbert only laughed and breathed heavily against her ear. "I am a wealthy man, my dear. I can see your father put out of business and driven from this place before you can so much as scream."

Jeanine realized that she was treading dangerous water. She thought frantically for how she might soothe the man's anger, without yielding to his demands. "Monsieur, I am but a simple maiden. I have no mind for such matters, but it is my understanding that you and my father have an agreement most binding by the laws of our land. I do not doubt that you are a powerful man."

At this he laughed and pressed his body closer still. "I am a very powerful man."

Jeanine fought to keep her emotions from revealing themselves on her face. She glanced upward, nearly faint from the foul smell of the man's breath. "You surely would not wish for people in the village to say you go back on your word. Breaking faith with my father would not bode well for your reputation."

"My dear Jeanine," he said, his wet lips perilously close to her own mouth, "I intend on breaking faith with no one. I have come, in fact, that the agreement might be completed sooner than expected."

Jeanine easily realized that she had led him in the wrong direction. It was her desire to put an end to their betrothal, not hasten its conclusion. "But monsieur, I do not wish to be a wife to you."

"I care not," he replied quite matter-of-factly. "Your desires and wishes are of little importance. You will be my wife, and you will give me many fine sons." He lowered his mouth to hers, just as Jeanine turned her face. The slobbery wet lips fell only upon her cheek, yet even this made her feel ill. Violently, she twisted against his hold and tried to push him from her.

"You forget yourself, monsieur!" she declared, but Colbert was ruthless in his pursuit.

Not standing a chance against him, Jeanine thought of screaming as he put his thick hand to her throat. "Be still, or I'll give you a beating you won't forget."

She froze in fear. "You are not my husband. You have no right."

"Ah, but I soon will be, and there is nothing you can do

to prevent your fate. Now I demand a kiss, and should you resist, I will remember this day upon our wedding night and exact my revenge quite thoroughly."

Jeanine was at a loss, and Colbert took her silent contemplation as acceptance. He kissed her roughly and ran his hand along her neck and down her shoulder.

"What is this? Monsieur, you forget yourself," Margarite de la Fontaine said as she swept into the room.

Colbert pulled away, his gaze defying Jeanine to say one word against him. "I was overcome by your daughter's beauty," he said, turning to smile at Margarite.

Jeanine's mother looked unconvinced that such an excuse was reasonable for the liberties she'd just witnessed. "Monsieur, she is but a maid. You will frighten her with such bold advances. Please," she paused to motion him to the fire, "come sit here and woo her gently."

Jeanine grimaced behind Colbert's back. She wished with all her heart that she might soundly club the man over the head. Just then he turned and smiled as if reading her thoughts. Jeanine drew in a sharp breath. He reached out his hand to take hold of her arm. "Let us do as your mother bids."

"But, ma *mère,* have you forgotten? We are expecting a guest. A very ill guest," Jeanine said, straining to pull away.

"Our guest will not require your attention," her mother said in an anxious voice. Her eyes seemed to warn Jeanine not to upset Colbert.

Jeanine suddenly realized the desperation of her plight. She could not further injure Antoine Colbert without her family falling prey to some retribution for her actions. Quietly she allowed the offensive man to lead her to the bench by the fire.

"Madame de la Fontaine," Colbert began, "you must

persuade your husband to shorten the time before our vows. I long to take your daughter to my home—to make her my beloved wife—to see her happy."

Those three things can never coexist, Jeanine thought grimly as he continued his plea.

"I have cared for your daughter from afar, and now that your husband has agreed to the contract of marriage, I see it as foolishness to continue this lengthy waiting period."

Jeanine's mother shrugged. "Monsieur, I cannot speak for my husband. His word is law in our home."

Colbert nodded. "As it should be. I only ask that you might influence him a bit. Perhaps I could even sweeten the pot, say by adding additional funds to be disbursed for your pleasure?"

"Monsieur, you would find your answer only with my husband."

"*Oui,* but a beautiful woman often holds sway over those caught up in her spell."

"It doesn't seem to be helping me any," Jeanine muttered.

Colbert tightened his hold on her arm and sat down, drawing her with him. Jeanine was caught off balance and nearly landed on his lap. Colbert only chuckled. "See?" he questioned, looking upward to catch her mother's horrified expression. "She already longs to be near me."

Jeanine tried to add distance to the space between them, but Colbert held her fast. "Talk to your husband, madame. See if he won't see things my way. 'Twould be most beneficial for your family."

Casting her daughter an apologetic look before curtsying, Madame de la Fontaine responded, "I will do as you ask."

Colbert nodded. "Good. Then leave us to make our wedding plans."

Jeanine knew her mother was in no position to argue.

The older woman left the room with a look of panic that made Jeanine's heartache only worsen. How dare Colbert come into their home and treat her mother so disrespectfully? But then, the law gave him full right. They were indebted to Colbert, and without his generous offer to resolve their debt, Jeanine had little trouble believing he would see them all thrown into prison.

With her mother gone, Jeanine wondered what he might try next. She dared a glance and found him watching her.

"Milord?"

"It is my opinion that you are the fairest creature in all of Flanders," he said in a near breathless manner. "I find I hunger for you and that my hunger must be satisfied. Think not that you will escape my plans for you. No other will have you, Jeanine de la Fontaine. You will belong to me for all time. Now and always."

Jeanine shuddered. *Dear Lord God,* she prayed, *do not let it be so.*

five

Jeanine felt immense relief when Colbert took his leave. He mentioned attending to some affair of state and said it was the only thing that could tear him from her side. She ran for the water bucket after his departure and scrubbed her face and arms where the touch of Colbert left her feeling tainted. It was while doing this that she heard her father and brother struggling up the back stairs.

"Père?" she called, casting a glance over the landing rail.

"Oui," he grunted. He precariously balanced the weight of a litter between his bulky shoulders, while Étienne, standing several steps above his father, was nearly bent in half in order to keep the litter even.

Jeanine dared a glance at the litter, and her breath caught in her throat. Victor Pindar was staring up at her with an expression something between pain and confusion. "I have the room already prepared, *Père,*" Jeanine said.

Again her father grunted, but he said nothing until they had managed to gain entry onto the second floor. "Go, make clear the way," her father ordered, and Jeanine fairly danced to do his bidding.

She called to her mother, announcing the arrival of Monsieur Pindar, then pushed back the door to her room and stood aside as her father and brother carried Victor to her bed. Once they had settled him on top of the clean linens, Jeanine went to work to make him comfortable.

"Are you warm enough, monsieur?" she asked, bringing yet another thick wool blanket.

44

"I am fine," Victor managed to say. He lifted his gaze to Étienne. "You are most gracious to see to my needs. I will one day repay this debt."

"Then pay it back to my sister. To tell you honestly, I was much consumed by the damage done my ship. I fear I left you to the care of others without much more than a brief thought," Étienne admitted. "Jeanine pointed out the error of my ways."

Victor turned ever so slightly to catch Jeanine's intent study. "Thank you, mademoiselle. You were most kind to suggest such care."

Jeanine smiled. " 'Tis our Christian duty to see to our fellow man, *n'est-ce pas?*"

"Indeed it is so, daughter," her father stated. "Now, I suspect this young man would be in need of rest."

"And I have brought just the healing balm to bring about such a thing," Margarite de la Fontaine said, entering the room. She held out a draught of thick dark liquid.

Victor took the mug, downed the contents, then smiled ever so slightly. " 'Tis not nearly so bitter as that which the good doctor prescribed."

Jeanine laughed at the thought of Simon's concoction. "Medicine was not intended to taste good, but to make one feel good or at least better. Mother has a way with herbs, and no doubt you will be quite satisfied with her abilities."

"No doubt," Victor said, nodding acknowledgment to Madame de la Fontaine.

"Come now, let us leave the man in peace. He should sleep well here tonight," Jeanine's father said. Turning to Victor, he added, "And should you need anything, one of us will be close at hand."

"Oui," Jeanine said, turning to gather up several things. " 'Twill be my place to sleep outside your door. Just call

to me for any help you might need. My name is Jeanine."

What had started out seeming the perfect solution to her problems gave Jeanine little satisfaction. Victor seemed not in the leastwise interested in her ministrations. She cared for him daily, taking an interest in anything that had to do with him. She had even gained the raised eyebrow of her mother by offering to bathe Victor two days after his arrival. That suggestion was quickly dismissed, and instead Madame de la Fontaine attended to that need. Nevertheless, Jeanine maintained hope that somehow she could convince Victor to fall in love with her. Or at least take a marginal interest in her.

Sitting at his bedside on the fourth day of Victor's stay, Jeanine realized that nearly another week had passed, moving her ever closer to becoming Antoine Colbert's wife. She grimaced as she worked her needlepoint. There seemed no hope of escaping the inevitable.

"That color must hurt your eyes," Victor said, rather groggily.

Jeanine's head snapped up to find him watching her. "Why do you say that?"

"You could not imagine the expression on your face," he replied and eased himself up a bit in the bed.

Jeanine dropped her sewing and helped him to sit up against the headboard. She liked the feel of his warm arms against her hands and the way the muscles became hard and firm as he worked to push himself up. He was used to hard work, she decided, and yet he seemed very much to take on the part of the wealthy nobleman. He spoke French in perfect order and seemed most intelligent, yet he didn't take on airs with her or her family.

As she bent over him to pull the pillow into position, Jeanine found that her face was only inches from his. She froze, finding her gaze drawn to his. For a moment, neither one said anything, and Jeanine felt her breath catch in her throat. Victor's dark eyes beheld her with almost amused interest. His face fascinated Jeanine in a way that she could not explain. It caused her to commit to memory every line and wrinkle, but mostly it caused her heart to beat faster and her palms to grow moist.

"I suppose this is some new manner of care," he finally said. "You are breathing your breath into me, willing over your health to my body, is that it?"

Jeanine startled at such a thought and straightened up quickly. "I. . .I. . .am. . .sorry." She felt her face grow hot with embarrassment. She went quickly to retrieve her sewing and pricked her finger three times before giving up the pretense. When she glanced up she found Victor still studying her.

"So how is that you are still in your father's house?" he questioned her finally. "You look old enough to be wed and caring for several babes."

Jeanine felt even more embarrassment over this reference to her age. She toyed with the idea of remaining silent or even of changing the subject, but since this was the most attention Victor had ever offered her, she was eager to answer. "I am very old. I am twenty. But I've been useful to my parents," she replied, not knowing what else to say.

Victor smiled ever so slightly and rubbed his stubbly chin. "Yes, I can well imagine."

He continued to stare at her, and Jeanine, not knowing what else to do, decided to turn the conversation in another direction. "What are transepts?" she asked.

"Where in the world did you hear that term?" he asked, eyeing her oddly.

Jeanine suddenly realized that the only time she'd ever heard the word was while Victor was delirious and under the care of Dr. Font. She felt momentarily frantic to think up an excuse, but none would come. "I don't know," she lied. "I think I heard some men talking one day. I thought to ask my father, but I forgot and thought perhaps you might know."

He continued to study her in silence as if deciding whether she should be privy to such knowledge. His look made her uneasy, and Jeanine instantly dropped her gaze to her handwork.

"A transept is the extended part of a cathedral that crosses and separates the nave from the choir," he finally answered.

"Nave? Choir? You mean the singers?" she asked, forgetting her earlier embarrassment.

He grinned. "Not exactly. 'Tis a term for architects, those builders of cathedrals. The nave is the portion of the building where you stand in worship during the services." Jeanine nodded as if visualizing it in her mind. "The nave usually has robing rooms or chapels on either side of the main room. The choir is that portion at the front of the church and on the other side of the transept, which is nearest the altar. Understand?"

"Yes, thank you. Are you an architect?" she asked boldly. Her need to know more about him outweighed her concern that he might question her intrusion into his privacy.

"Actually, yes." He looked thoughtful for a moment.

"And have you built such a cathedral?" she asked.

"You are most perceptive," he answered, turning slightly and wincing as he did.

"You should not move without help," she offered, starting to get up from her chair. "Your ribs are broken."

He waved her back. " 'Tis unnecessary. I grow stronger every day thanks to the care of your family and my good physicians."

"Yes, I heard from my brother that you were nearly dead when they took you from the ship." Jeanine wondered what if anything he remembered of his ordeal at Simon's.

" 'Twould seem true enough," he answered and relaxed against the headboard of her bed.

Jeanine liked the way his disheveled hair hung down onto his forehead and across his right eye. When he reached up to push it back, she longed to touch it as well. She couldn't resist wondering what it might feel like against her fingers. Unpleasant memories of Antoine Colbert's grease-laden hair made her shudder.

"Are you cold?" Victor suddenly asked.

Jeanine's thoughts were brought back in line. "Nay, I was just imaging how terrible a storm at sea might be." Again she lied, and her conscience began to sorely bother her. She seemed to bring falsehoods into every walk of her life.

"It was a bad storm," Victor agreed. " 'Twas our good fortune that your brother is the seaman he is. He risked his life more than once for his men, and I hold him in the highest regard. Of course some things could not be helped. The waves were fierce and there were several men washed overboard. But your brother did what he could."

Jeanine beamed a smile at this. "Aye, he is a good man. A loving soul who deserves much more than he has. I would like to see him find a good woman to marry. With his infinite patience he would make a wonderful father."

Victor raised a dark brow as if contemplating whether this might be true. The silence fell awkwardly between them, and Jeanine sought to think of a topic. Then memory served her another reminder, and it seemed the perfect thing. "Do you have a brother?"

"Non," Victor answered. "I have a dear sister and nephew, but no one else. My sister lives in England, and

when I am in England, I live with her and her little boy, Marcus."

"What is her name?" Jeanine asked, knowing full well the answer.

"Eleanor. Lady Eleanor Bramston. She has a wonderful estate outside of Dover. Her husband died some time back, and now she keeps the lands for her son."

"Are you close?"

"Aye," Victor said softly. "As close as two people can be."

Jeanine felt an instantaneous envy for the woman. His obvious admiration for his sister made her wish he might feel something half so strong for her. But Victor seemed to show absolutely no interest in her whatsoever. He seemed equally content whether she came to offer him care, or her mother came in her stead. It didn't appear to matter who kept him company, nor in fact, whether he had any company at all.

"I had your father send her word of my recovery," Victor finally added. "I could not bear to think of her fretting over my well-being."

"You are most thoughtful," Jeanine said. "Most men would not consider the feelings of a woman to be worth much."

Victor looked at her as if she had spoken some hideous lie. "A man of honor and valor would," he said flatly, almost as if challenging her to deny it.

She smiled weakly and pretended to pick at her embroidery thread. "Then there is a short supply of such men in Flanders."

Victor chuckled at this. It was apparent he had taken no real offense at her words. "Mayhap you should visit England."

Jeanine looked up and smiled. "Mayhap I should."

In her guise as Dr. Font, Jeanine tried hard to put her mind from Victor and turn to the studies at hand. Finding it nearly impossible to concentrate, Jeanine looked at the words in the book until her vision blurred.

"I am thinking your mind is not entirely with us this day," Simon said, suddenly leaning back in his chair.

Jeanine attempted a smile. "I suppose it isn't."

"And might this have something to do with our patient, Monsieur Pindar?"

"It might." Jeanine lifted her gaze to meet Simon's grandfatherly regard.

"So, our study of humors and apothecary treatments is of little interest in comparison—eh?"

"Non," she said, shaking her head. " 'Tis not a lack of interest, I assure you."

"Very well, then let us continue." Simon pointed to a sketch of the brain. "Tell me of the humors related here."

"Phlegm," Jeanine replied. "This humor is associated with the brain, and is represented by water, because it is cold and moist. Treatments are used to either reduce the heat of fevers or to induce the moisture in order to aid the humor."

"Good, and this?"

"Blood, associated with the heart," she nearly sighed the latter word. "It is hot and moist and represented by air." *Or Victor Pindar,* her own heart told her.

They passed quickly through a recitation of the other two humors—yellow and black bile. Jeanine listened with half-hearted interest as Simon reviewed the information that a good balance of all humors was called *eukrasia,* while an imbalanced body was said to be in a state of *dyskrasia.*

"Now let us discuss the remedies at hand that we might use in the treatment of the body," Simon suggested.

"What of dill?"

Jeanine frowned and tried to remember everything she could associate with dill. "It is warm and dry with usefulness for relieving a cold and windy stomach. It can be harmful to the kidneys and is best taken with the juice of a lemon."

"Good. And oil of almonds?"

"Warm in the second degree and moist. Helpful for the chest and for coughs. Too much can damage weak intestines, but overall it generates moderate humors and is useful in temperate bodies."

"And ricotta?" Simon pressed her to concentrate.

Jeanine shifted uncomfortably. "Cold and humid. Best obtained from pure milk. Good for fattening up the body." She thought of Victor Pindar and her care of him while with Simon. She remembered testing his broken ribs and finding that there wasn't an ounce of fat to mar his frame. How very unlike Antoine Colbert, who apparently indulged in ricotta at will.

Simon eyed her critically. "You aren't listening."

"I am sorry," she said, softly. "My mind is greatly consumed."

"With a certain young man, no doubt."

She felt her face flush. "Why do you say that?"

"Because I know you too well, Dr. Font." Simon closed his apothecary study. "So how is Monsieur Pindar?"

"He is well. Amazingly so. His scalp has healed nicely and there seems to be no bad effect from the trephining." She was eager to discuss Victor, and it showed. Showed so much in fact, that Simon began to laugh. "What?" Jeanine questioned.

"Methinks this topic is of much greater interest than the others."

Jeanine let out a heavy sigh. "You know me far too well,

Simon. How is it that you see through me so readily?"

"You wear your heart on your sleeve, my dear *docteur*." He gave her a knowing smile. "Yours and monsieur's."

"Would that I could have his heart," she said rather miserably.

"For dissection, no doubt," Simon teased. "A thing which all comely wenches desire."

Jeanine looked up in surprise. She had never heard Simon talk in such a manner and said so.

"But then, I've never needed to deal with you as a love-sick ninny," he said in a rather sympathetic tone. "You have given your heart to this man, *non?*"

"I'm afraid so," she said, knowing the dejection in her tone would not be missed by her mentor.

"And this is bad?"

"Not in and of itself." She looked away, then eased her elbows onto the table and leaned her face in her hands.

"Then why such an expression on so beautiful a face?"

Jeanine laughed. "Ashes and mud become me, eh?"

"There is beauty that no disguise may hide. But you have not answered my question. Why is there such despair in realizing that you have given your heart to a man?"

" 'Tis not the giving that is of despairing nature," Jeanine admitted. "But I fear that my heart has very much been returned. He could not possibly be less interested in me."

"I find that hard to believe. How could any man reject so lovely a creature?"

Jeanine smiled. "You are kind, Simon, but I'm afraid I had more attention from him as Dr. Font. Although, we did have a nice conversation yesterday morning. 'Twas my hope he might have found favor in me, but I was mistaken."

"And what makes you so certain of this?"

"When I returned later that afternoon, he waved me off and wished to be left to his letter writing. That sister of his is all that he concerns himself with."

Simon reached out and touched her arm. "You must never despair. God has a purpose in this."

"A purpose in breaking my heart?" Jeanine asked quite seriously.

"Perhaps it is not so much breaking that He has in mind, as it is preparation."

Jeanine sat back and shook her head. "No, Victor has no interest in me, whatsoever. And in two weeks I am to marry Antoine Colbert."

"A grave problem, to be sure."

"I am doomed," she said sadly, wishing she could find hope in their conversation.

"You must pray about this and seek God's heart. His eye is upon you and He attendeth all mankind, so think yourself not included if that is your wish, but 'twould be a lie."

Jeanine smiled. "I suppose you are right. I will pray about it and seek His will, but I hope He will answer before two weeks are concluded."

"God has his own timing," Simon assured her. " 'Tis never too late, nor too early. Wait patiently for Him, Jeanine, and He will direct your steps."

six

Antoine Colbert shifted uncomfortably on his gouty foot, all the while watching the book copy shop of Simon Grosz. For the last week he'd found Jeanine's daily foray into the dock district a perplexity of grand proportions. Why did she journey to the this place, day after day? Better still, why did she spend hours within the rundown walls after her arrival? Unable to put off a personal exploration any longer, Colbert tightened his hold on his purse strings and hobbled painfully across the busy street to the shop.

Entering the darkened room, Colbert called out. "Good day!"

Simon appeared, wiping his hands on a towel. "Greetings, good sir, and how might I assist you?"

This created a moment of confusion for Colbert, who was uncertain what he should ask of the old man. Just as he took a step, however, his gouty foot caused him to nearly fall forward. He grimaced in pain, and Simon seemed to immediately understand.

"Your foot grieves you. Come this way and the doctor will consider it."

"The doctor?" Colbert questioned.

Simon laughed. "Oh, but you thought it to be me. But of course, I am a physician. My eyes, however, are bad. Dr. Font will see to your need."

"Dr. Font," Colbert whispered. He allowed Simon to help him into a chair. Bringing a stool, Simon elevated the man's aching foot and admonished him to remain still.

"The doctor is finishing with another patient, but 'tis certain your wait will not be long."

"Very well," Colbert replied.

He sat for some moments contemplating the room in which Simon had left him. It appeared to be some manner of sleeping quarters. Two crudely built beds edged up against one wall, while a counter of weather-beaten wood held a tray of assorted, indistinguishable instruments. The inner room was dark except for the warming glow that spilled out from the fireplace, and the entire house smelled of something Antoine could not quite place.

"I am told your foot is giving you trouble," a smallish man said, entering the room with a trident-styled candlestick holder. The flames flickered from atop the tapers as the man moved to place it across the room. Pausing beside the tray of instruments, the doctor seemed completely absorbed with his task.

Colbert watched him closely. With the man's back to him, Colbert could distinguish nothing but black robes and a bit of graying black hair at the edge of his cap. The man stood of slight build, but seemed most determined in his duties. Colbert wondered what this man might know of Jeanine and opened his mouth to ask that very question when the man turned and stared at him in surprise. The clattering of the metallic instrument against the wooden floor echoed loudly in the silent room.

Huge brown eyes, eyes that had widened in fear at him on every occasion of greeting, now stared back from the ash-smudged face. Jeanine!

"What are you doing here?" Colbert questioned, rage evident in his tone.

"I. . .I. . ." she stammered, unable to answer him.

He got to his feet, forgetting his pain, and came to where Jeanine de la Fontaine stood. Dragging the cap from her head, he instantly saw the carefully sewn strip that contained the coarse dark hair. "What game is this?" He studied the cap for several moments as if trying to force the object itself to answer.

"Monsieur Colbert." She barely breathed the name as he dropped the cap and yanked her around to pull at her tightly pinned hair.

"Answer me! What game is this?" The thick braid came free in his hands and the luxurious silken mane begged his touch.

" 'Tis no game," Jeanine said in a whimper. She seemed frozen in place as Colbert ran his fingers through the braid, loosening the tight weave until Jeanine's curly hair spilled out across his open hand.

He turned her again, and this time tightly held her while he shook her most severely. "It looks to be nothing but a game. Why are you here and dressed thusly?"

Simon took this moment to return to the room and stared in stunned disbelief at the scene before him. "What are you about, my good man?" he asked Colbert. "Unhand the good doctor."

" 'Tis no doctor I hold. This is my betrothed. I'm alarmed to find her parading in men's garments and pretending to be a physician. I want to know why, and I want to know now." He tightened his hold. "Answer me or I'll burn this place down around us!" He watched, gloating under the intimidated expressions on the faces of his opponents.

"Monsieur, you are hurting me," Jeanine protested, struggling to free herself.

"I will do more than that if you do not tell me the truth." He could see the fear on her face and felt a certain victory in the way she trembled. He had longed to make her tremble after him in another fashion, but at present this was most gratifying. He thought again of her father's bargain and how within a fortnight she'd be his to control. She'd no doubt fight him then as well, but it would all be for naught. He'd have her as his wife, and he'd take control of her life from that moment on.

"Please, monsieur!" Jeanine begged.

"She must disguise herself in order to help the poor," Simon offered, but Colbert paid him no attention. He stared into the haunted eyes of the small woman instead.

"I am a physician," Jeanine said. "Please let me go." Her eyes implored him to set her free, but Colbert was greedy for her.

"You practice the art of medicine when you know it is forbidden?" he asked in a low whisper. She nodded very slowly and fearfully. He smiled. "I could have you killed for this. I could have you put before the church and condemned as a witch. You know that, do you not?"

"Please, monsieur, she is very good to the people around her. They cannot afford another doctor, and so they come to her," Simon offered by way of explanation.

"She is to be my wife!" Colbert growled the declaration and finally dropped his hold. He studied the trembling woman before him. "This is most unacceptable, my dear Jeanine. You have long kept secrets from me, but this is a most delicate matter which must be handled immediately. We will go now and be married. Our elopement is the only answer in order to save face."

"You must be mad!" Jeanine declared and moved back several paces—her gaze locked on his face. "I have no desire to marry you now or ever. 'Tis the truth I've told you at every turn. My practice here is no secret to those who seek my care. The secret comes in that men like yourself refuse me the right to practice openly. I am a good physician."

"Aye, I well imagine that you are. But a physician of

what? Broken hearts? What manner of woman have you become, my dear Jeanine?"

"Sir, I protest your implications of her character," Simon inserted. "Mademoiselle de la Fontaine is of impeccable virtue. She is kindhearted and given to sharing the love of God with her people. Fault her not for seeing their pain and suffering and deciding to do something in order to put an end to it. If you would but—"

"Enough!" Colbert shouted, turning to Simon. "And who are you that you should have such a thing go on behind these walls? I own a great deal of property in this town. I am a powerful man. One word from me will see you driven from this village without a single soul to mourn your passing. The ruination of this woman will be upon your shoulders."

" 'Tis untrue," Jeanine said, completely enraged. She went to stand beside her friend. "Simon is a good man, and many would mourn his passing. I, for one, would be quite lost without Simon, and he has done nothing to compromise my reputation."

Colbert yanked his intended away from the side of the strange little man. No doubt he was of foreign birth, which made Colbert even happier to see to his disposal. Foreigners were gradually increasing in numbers around the small town, and Colbert would be quite happy to see them driven out. Never mind that they boosted the otherwise sagging economy of Bruges and had allowed for an expansion. He despised them all. "You are not of our people, are you?" Colbert asked, eyeing Simon suspiciously. The question was nearly an accusation in and of itself. Jeanine tried to place herself between the two men, but Colbert drew her back so sharply that she stumbled and fell.

"No," Simon admitted, grimacing at the rough treatment Colbert inflicted upon Jeanine. "I was born many miles to the east and am of the Hebrew faith."

"A Jew!" Colbert exclaimed. "I should have recognized the stench."

"Antoine!" Jeanine cried, using his given name. She managed to get to her feet and put herself at Colbert's side.

Colbert smiled with an evil leer. " 'Tis the first time you have called me by that name. I like the way it sounds upon your lips. Particularly when it rings with pleadings for my mercy."

Jeanine swallowed hard, and Colbert could tell that she fought with herself against speaking out too quickly. "I am pleading mercy for this man. He is a good man of no consequence to you. I will leave this place, but you needn't punish Simon for something he is not guilty of."

"He is a Jew practicing medicine. The laws of the land make it quite clear this is a punishable offense. His guilt or innocence is for a court to decide. But as for you. . ." Colbert reached out and with one fluid motion rent the black houppeland Jeanine used for her doctoring duties.

Gasping, Jeanine clutched at the garment in spite of the heavy linen chemise that she wore beneath the robe. "How dare you!"

"I dare because you belong to me." He leaned close, enjoying the pleasant scent of her. "You would do well to remember that. Be there a ring on your finger and words made before a priest or not, you are contracted to me, and I will see this thing through in prompt order. But for now, I want you out of that offensive costume and properly clothed immediately. I will not have the town folk see you in your shame."

Jeanine nodded hesitantly and went to the changing room, while Simon stepped forward to issue his own thoughts. "You, monsieur, must understand. God has blessed Jeanine with the ability to heal the sick. Why should this be of offense to you?"

"It is of offense to me because she is a woman, and she need not soil her hands in such a manner. It offends me because in the eyes of the church and the laws of this good land it is illegal for her to practice such a position. Women are incapable of such complicated thought."

"But she—"

Colbert slapped Simon hard across the face. "Silence, Jew. You have obviously interfered enough in this matter. You have corrupted her, and I will see you put in prison."

"No!" Jeanine declared, coming from the changing room, still trying to secure her belt. "Simon is a good man." Her hair flew out wildly behind her.

Colbert grabbed her by both arms and moved his face to within inches of hers. "I will not brook disobedience, woman."

"Please do not hurt her," Simon said, coming to put a hand on Colbert's shoulder.

The mere touch enraged Colbert. How dare this sniveling little Jew touch him and defile him in such a way! Dropping his hold on Jeanine, he gave Simon the back of his hand, sending the man sprawling onto the floor. Simon clutched first his face and then his chest as the look of shock changed to one of fierce pain.

"Come along, mademoiselle," Colbert said, taking Jeanine in hand.

Simon gasped for breath and moaned.

"No," Jeanine said, fighting against Colbert's grasp. "Cannot you see? He is hurt, mayhap even dying. He needs me."

"I care not. The man may rot for all I care." He tightened his hold and pushed her toward the door.

"Please, Antoine, let me see to him."

Colbert pulled her out the door and onto the street. "He

is a Jew. If you must care for someone, come care for me, my dear. In but a few short hours you shall have your hands filled with all that you need pay attention to." He laughed mercilessly as she attempted to flee him. It was good to finally have the upper hand where the wench was concerned. She'd put him off for far too long, and now he would have his way. Even her father wouldn't be able to refuse his demands.

seven

"Jeanine should have been home hours ago," Margarite de la Fontaine said with a definite look of worry. She tried to busy herself with the dried herbs she would use for their dinner, but it was obviously of little help.

Étienne shrugged his shoulders. " 'Tis her way to be out and about the town. Mayhap she has taken herself to the grave of our grandmother. Would you wish that I go in search of her?"

His mother nodded. "Please."

Étienne smiled tolerantly and kissed her on the forehead. "If it gives your mind peace, then so it will be. Please tell my father where I have gone when he comes in from tending the animals."

Again his mother nodded.

Étienne, dressed in a blue tunic and cotehardie that reached just below his red-hose-clad thighs, strode in long easy steps down the main street of Bruges. His little sister was often given over for her fanciful flights, but he could see the worry in his mother's face and would soundly chide Jeanine for her thoughtlessness this time.

He began to whistle a tune, finding it a perfect day to be out. In another fortnight he would be back upon the sea, his first and only love. He had already decided that if the stilting of the river was impossible to reverse or control, he would move to Calais or Antwerp and continue with shipping from there. At least in Antwerp, the trade was good and the crossroads of several overland routes past through the city. Added to this, the River Scheldt showed

63

no signs of silting. Étienne had tried to convince his father
to settle his debts and leave Bruges behind, but he knew it
would be difficult at best for the man to uproot himself
after living a lifetime in the city.

Étienne smiled to himself. His father was a sensible
man. There would come an answer to him in one form or
another. There always did. And when the answer came to
François de la Fontaine, they would join together to see
the thing brought into existence. His father was just that
way. So, too, was his sister, and Étienne nearly laughed
aloud at the thought of Jeanine taking up the banner of
moving the family to Antwerp. No doubt she'd have them
all packed and ready to board one of the family ships
before their father even knew what was happening.

Rounding the corner little more than two blocks from
the de la Fontaine home and business, Étienne stopped in
his tracks. Gone were the pleasantries of the day. Just
ahead, Antoine Colbert approached with Jeanine most
attentively clutching his arm.

"And what might the meaning of this be?" Étienne asked,
seeing a sudden panic in the eyes of his sister.

"Ah, there is much that you have a right to know,"
Colbert answered without allowing Jeanine to explain. "But
we should do our talking in private. I am now come to do
just that. Lead the way, my good man, and I will explain
all."

"Étienne, he has some misguided notion—"

"Pay her no attention. The time has come that we can no
longer keep our secrets, my sweet," Colbert interrupted,
and Étienne watched as the man threw Jeanine a leering
grin. "After all, some secrets refuse to be kept, eh?"

"I know not what you speak of," Jeanine declared, but
as if remembering they were on the common street, she
added, looking at her brother, "Let us go to our father, and

I will explain."

Étienne nodded, wondering what possible explanation the couple would offer. If Colbert's implications were of any merit, it could only mean one thing. And to imagine that made Étienne's blood boil within him. The couple lagged behind him, and glancing back, Étienne watched as Colbert whispered into Jeanine's ear. She seemed to pale, then nodded most vigorously in agreement to whatever he had suggested. Étienne knew something must surely be amiss, for he'd never known his sister to comply willingly with anything Colbert suggested. Perhaps she had realized the futility of fighting the contract. Or mayhap—and Étienne found this almost impossible to believe—his sister had gained some manner of feeling for Colbert which differed from the hatred she had always conveyed in the past.

&

"I'm not entirely certain that I understand," François de la Fontaine said, eyeing his daughter, scrutinizing her for the truth. They were gathered together on the second floor, near to the exact spot where they had finalized the arrangements for the betrothal.

Colbert refused to allow Jeanine to talk. It was under the threat of completely destroying her family and of seeing Simon dead, if he were not already in that state, that Colbert had insisted she remain silent while he explained.

"I know 'tis my own doing," Colbert began, "but in truth, such deception was not my plan from the beginning. Jeanine and I simply forgot ourselves."

Jeanine grimaced and lowered her head. She knew it appeared that she was too burdened with her shame to consider the faces of her family, but in truth she was outraged. How dare he lie to her father?

Then a horrible thought came to her. For years she had lied to her entire family. Telling them that she was out to visit one friend or another while hurrying to hide herself and her identify, all in order to practice medicine. This caused her yet another pain-filled thought. Not only had she lied to her parents, but she had broken the law. Consumed with guilt, Jeanine thought perhaps she was receiving exactly what she deserved.

"These past weeks have been a trying time for the both of us," Colbert said with mock humility. "I'm afraid your daughter has not gone in truth to visit her friends, but rather has made her way every day to meet. . ." He paused as if to force Jeanine's attention.

Her head snapped up to meet his expression. Would he tell them the truth? Would he put Simon's life in jeopardy? Oh, that the earth would open up and swallow her whole. She bit her lower lip and looked away. There was nothing she could do about that which he would say.

Colbert smiled evilly. "Jeanine came to meet me. I'm afraid it is now most imperative that we marry immediately."

Jeanine brought her openmouthed gaze back to his cruel, self-assured expression. He had just implied their intimacy. He hadn't implicated Simon, but he'd ruined her just the same. Her mother began to weep, while her father stared at the couple as if trying to decide the truth of the matter. Surely, Jeanine thought, even if he believed such a thing were true he would remember her disdain for Colbert and believe him capable of forcing the intimacy between them. *But there was no intimacy,* Jeanine's mind raged. How dare he imply that she had soiled herself with him? He, whose very countenance sickened her. Confusion filled her mind. How could she manage to refrain from further lies to cover the ones she'd already told.

"Are you telling me that my daughter is with child?" François de la Fontaine asked sternly.

At this Jeanine's mother sobbed and bit at her hand to

silence her anguish. Étienne looked at Jeanine with a hard stare of disappointment, while her father continued to meet the haughty look of Antoine Colbert. How could they believe such nonsense was true?

" 'Tis nothing new to this continent," Colbert offered offhandedly. "I still intend to marry the wench. It isn't as though I would desert her while she carries my babe in her belly. I merely thought it prudent to explain and see the wedding concluded on the morrow."

"And what say you for yourself, daughter?"

Jeanine met the eyes of her father and wanted to die. She longed to cry out in a voice of anguished protest that it was all a lie. Her life, Colbert's declarations, this circumstance. But she worried that Simon, poor Simon with his chest full of pain, would be exposed and put from Bruges or, worse yet, killed. How could she risk his life now? Mayhap he was already dead, but if not, she had to protect him, even at cost of her own disgrace. Then too, if she declared Colbert to be the scoundrel that he was, he would call her father's note due immediately and see him ruined.

Finally, with a heavy heart, Jeanine spoke. "You know well my heart, mon *père*. I have long wished to do that which is right in the eyes of our Lord God. But I have lied." There. She had done it. She had said just enough to leave little doubt in anyone's mind of her guilt. Turning to face Colbert, she refused to react to his smirking grin. "I will marry Monsieur Colbert on the morrow."

There was little else to be said. Her mother cried inconsolably, while her brother shook his head in disgust. Her father, once the light of her life, looked upon her as though she'd suddenly acquired the plague. Nay, with the plague she would have merited his pity and sympathy. His look of disgust mingled with bitter disappointment caused Jeanine's eyes to well with tears. If only she had never lied about her medicinal practices. If only she had long ago explained Simon to her parents and told them openly of her work with the poor.

"I believe the matter has settled itself," Colbert said confidently. "And to show my generosity, especially now that it is proven she is not barren, I will add yet another sum to our agreement."

Jeanine wanted to gag. He was blatantly carrying the lie a heartbreaking distance to insure that her parents not protest the speedy union. Feeling a wave of nausea when Colbert bent close, she had to force herself to keep from pulling away.

"Soon, my dear. Very soon you will be mine," he told her, while her father tried to comfort his wife.

"Monsieur, I would ask you to return in the morning. It is necessary that we have a time to converse among ourselves. I am greatly distressed that you would take advantage of one so innocent as my daughter. I had thought to trust you as a man of your word."

Colbert got to his feet and made a low sweeping bow. "I throw myself upon your mercy, monsieur, just as you threw yourself upon mine not so long ago." His voice was filled with sardonic overtones.

"Of course," François de la Fontaine said, barely able to form the words. "We will meet again on the morrow."

Colbert shot Jeanine a look of victory and hobbled off toward the stairs. Jeanine thought for a moment about his gout, wondering if he'd sought any real treatment for the problem, when her father's low question roused her thoughts.

"How could you shame this house in such a manner?"

Jeanine was mindless of the question, having spied Victor Pindar as he made his slow, labored descent down the stairs. Her father seemed not to care that the stranger would hear his tirade and Jeanine's shame.

"Answer me!" her father said, pounding his fist against the small wooden table.

"I meant not to shame anyone," Jeanine replied softly. "I had hoped to explain, but it seems the words of another are weighed more heavily than mine."

Victor watched her with an odd expression on his face. She wished only to run from the room or to jump up, declaring her innocence. But nothing she said now was going to change the future. Colbert would see Simon driven from Bruges if she dared to refuse him now. It was also possible that Simon was already dead. She had seen men suffer from the heart pains that had attacked Simon. Of course, without having been allowed to thoroughly examine the man, she had no way of knowing his ailment, but it appeared most grave. She tried to remember his ashen face and pain-filled expression as she faced her family and bore her shame.

"I was unwise to lie," she admitted. "But it was not my intent to bring shame upon this family." Then as if to ease her own conscience, she added, "After all, 'tis your contract, not mine."

Étienne shook his head in disgust. "You have grieved your mother most unforgivably."

"Non," François de la Fontaine said, holding up a hand to stop his son. "All can be forgiven. Your sister's humiliation will soon be quite apparent, and Monsieur Colbert is good to take her in spite of this. At least he has not refused to see after his affair. He could have just as easily left your sister to bear her child alone."

Jeanine found her gaze drawn uncontrollably to the face of Victor Pindar. He watched as though observing a play. His face was unemotionally observant, his expression unreadable. Jeanine felt her heart in her throat. *Oh, Father,* she prayed, *I have lied and I have sinned, but 'tis not the sin they think me capable of. I only sought to help the poor and afflicted.* She longed for escape.

"I cannot believe that you should do this thing after so completely convincing me that Monsieur Colbert was an abomination to you," her father continued. Jeanine started to open her mouth, but her father silenced her. "I am ashamed of you. Look around you and see the pain you have caused. You have broken with the commandments of our Lord. You have told falsehoods and have lain with a man who was not yet your husband. Take yourself from my sight and pray for your salvation."

Her father's harsh reprimand caused tears to stream from Jeanine's eyes. She longed to clear her name, but instead took herself upstairs. She had closed the door to her bedroom before remembering that it was now Victor's room. Victor. The very image of his expression in her memory caused her great pain. He no doubt thought her to be little better than a common dock woman.

"Father, this is most unfair," she whispered the prayer. "I cannot bear such shame. Nor can I face such a future with Monsieur Colbert."

Going to the foot of her bed, Jeanine reached underneath and pulled out a bag. 'Twould be a simple enough matter to slip away in the night. But a destination of protection eluded her. Where could she run that Colbert would not hunt her down and find her? And now that she was publicly shamed, who would receive her? Hearing voices on the stairs, she took the bag and hurried out of the room and up to the fourth floor where she had made herself a pallet during the time Victor had shared their home. A few of her belongings were arranged there also, and with little thought to their care, Jeanine pushed them into the bag and waited for night to bring sleep upon the house. She wouldn't wait to become the wife of that brute. No matter the cost, she would not marry Antoine Colbert.

Reclining on the pallet, Jeanine prayed fervently for forgiveness. "Oh, Lord God," she began, even as heaviness descended upon her. "I have sinned, and I am sorry. I have made lying a way of life. I have given false witness at every turn whenever it suited my purpose. But I did not think 'twould cause damage. I only sought to do good with my medical skills."

Hot tears trickled from her eyes. "It was wrong to lie, but it was all I felt I could do. To explain to them my interest in medicine seemed hopeless." With that single word spoken aloud, Jeanine instantly thought of her *grandmère's* gentle guidance. She had always admonished Jeanine that hope could consistently be found in choosing God's way over one's own way.

"I see my error, Lord," Jeanine admitted. "My mother has long taught me to seek forgiveness, but somehow I believed that a sin done for the purpose of a greater good was somehow not a sin at all. Now I see that I was wrong, and yet 'tis too late. The people I love are hurt by my faithlessness, and the one man I might truly love will never be mine because I must either flee this house or marry Antoine Colbert on the morrow.

"Forgive me, Lord God. Please forgive me." And in that instant, Jeanine knew she was forgiven. Not that it undid the wrong which had already been done, but it did ease the burden she had carried around with her.

The silence of the room seemed to wrap itself around her. It drew her into a cocoon of protection, beckoning her to let go of her worries and sleep. Quickly, Jeanine uttered up a prayer for Simon's health and safety. Then just as she began to doze, she prayed that Victor might not believe the worst of her.

eight

Jeanine awoke with a start. The room was silent and black. She sat up, struggling to clear her groggy mind. For a moment, she remembered Colbert and his actions, and for just as short a moment thought perhaps it had all been part of a bad dream. But upon throwing back her covers, she discovered an unknown bulk at her feet. The bag. It confirmed that her nightmare was quite real.

Getting to her feet, Jeanine had little idea of the hour, but regardless, it was time to go. She lit a single candle, gathered what few things of hers remained, and made her way gingerly down the creaking steps. She paused at the third-floor landing as if to whisper good-bye to her family. Then her eyes fell upon her own bedchamber door. Victor would always believe her guilty of her sins. How she wished that she could assure them all that she had never known Colbert in the manner to which he eluded. How she longed to find favor in her father's eyes one more time. Perhaps in time she would pen them a letter and explain all the details that had led to that moment when Colbert had announced her a woman without virtue.

She started for the stairs, but a sudden thought of articles yet unclaimed came to mind. The closed bedchamber door did little to reassure her that she might collect her things without causing further disgrace to herself or family, but her grandmother's brooch and combs were of immeasurable wealth to her. They were all she had left of her grandmother. All that physically existed, she reminded herself, for indeed, her grandmother had left her a legacy of stories

72

and tales from the days gone by. These would forever stay with Jeanine, even if the combs and brooch were beyond her reach.

She put her bag on the floor and pushed the door open very quietly. Leaving the candle outside and trusting her lifelong memories for her sight into the blackened room, she paused inside the threshold and waited to see if Victor's sleeping form would be disturbed by her entry. He didn't move. Cautiously, she went to the foot of the bed and opened her trunk. It groaned loudly, but was soon forgotten when a hand grabbed her from out of the pitch black void and encircled her wrist. She smothered a scream with her free hand.

"What are you doing?" Victor's voice questioned.

Jeanine panted for air. "I'm. . .sorry. . .if. . .I disturbed you. I had only thought to retrieve something from my trunk."

Victor let her go and went to the hearth where the dying embers barely gave off enough light to outline his form. He tossed several sticks of wood on the fire, causing the room immediately to grow light, and Jeanine could see clearly that Victor was grimacing in pain.

"Please, go back to bed. You are hurting yourself."

" 'Tis nothing more than these sore ribs," he said, rubbing a hand across his chest.

" 'Tis broken ribs that pain you," Jeanine corrected and motioned him to at least sit. "Please rest. I'm sorry for the disturbance, but now that I am here, I will get what I came for and be gone."

Victor said nothing, but watched her intently as she rummaged in the trunk. Jeanine tried not to be overly nervous. She found her grandmother's articles, then came upon a thick woolen shawl her mother had made her and took that up as well.

"You are leaving, are you not?"

Victor's question in the heavy silence between them, surprised Jeanine so that she found it impossible to hide her expression. "I. . .ah. . .I am preparing myself for my departure. That is true."

"But you aren't departing on the morrow, are you? You are leaving now."

Jeanine thought to lie to him, then decided there had been enough lies from her lips. Had she not spent time already in prayer, begging God's forgiveness for such a thing? She had even thought to confess the truth of her medical practice to her family, then decided it would be easier this way. At least by slipping away in the night, no one need further encounter her. No one else need be hurt by her mistakes.

"Well?" Victor's soft voice warmed her heart.

"Aye."

"But where will you go? Surely your condition will soon begin to show, and then what will you do?"

Jeanine could no longer bear the humiliation. It was bad enough that her father believed her to have joined herself with Colbert, but to allow this wonderful man whom she'd totally lost her heart to, to believe such a thing made her quite ill.

"I have no reason to fear, monsieur. I am not with child, nor have I ever been given to Monsieur Colbert in that manner."

"But he told your father—"

"I know," she said, sadly. " 'Tis a matter I cannot explain."

Victor got up from the bed and came to sit on the very end by the trunk. He studied her thoroughly for a moment before speaking. "You speak the truth—of this I'm certain."

Jeanine laughed bitterly. "For once. I fear my lies have caused this entire matter. I have learned a cruel lesson about covering one's actions with falsehoods."

"But you did not defend yourself against those lies."

"I could not then, nor can I now. There is much that I cannot say on the matter, but suffice it to be that I am taking care of the problem in my own fashion."

"By running away?"

She looked up into his eyes and lost herself for a moment. Why couldn't he have loved her? As quickly as that thought came to mind, Jeanine pushed it aside. What good would it have done if he had? Her father had signed a contract with Monsieur Colbert. It would matter very little whether Victor cared for her or not. The agreement was most binding. It was this thought that caused Jeanine to sink to her knees.

"What will happen to my father?" she questioned softly.

Victor's expression betrayed his confusion. "What do you mean?"

"After I am gone."

"So you are intent upon leaving?"

"I have to. I despise Colbert. He has pursued me at every turn and has ruined my reputation before my family, all in order to have his own way. I cannot remain here to become his wife."

"I see," Victor replied and seemed to consider the situation. "I take it your father owes the man quite heavily?"

"Aye. The river silt has caused his shipping trade to be greatly reduced. He borrowed money and had hoped to make enough to pay Colbert back upon my brother's return, but alas that is not to be the case. The ship upon which you were injured required all extra monies in order to see it repaired. Soon the river trade here will be dead, and then Bruges will be dependent upon flat-bottomed boats or land routes. My brother has even talked of moving to Calais or Antwerp, but I'm certain my father would never hear of it for himself. Colbert offered to take me in trade. No woman of reputable means would have the man, and he needs heirs to secure his fortune for the future. The women who could be bought are not the type he would present as a wife, and those of purer means would not take a vow with him for any price."

"You included."

"Aye. I worry, though. I know my father has signed an agreement with Colbert. I worry over what will happen to him. Have you any thought on the matter?"

Victor shook his head. "No. I suppose 'tis a matter for the courts and Colbert to decide."

"Then no doubt they will see him sent to prison. Oh, why must this be so?" she said, wearily. It mattered little that she was on the point of breaking down completely. Victor had already seen her humiliated before her family. What did it matter that he saw her like this now?

"Mayhap they will only see you as a frightened bride and hold off on action for a time while they decide what has become of you," Victor offered.

"Mayhap. If only I had the money to give over that my father might pay his debts. Surely then, the court would dissolve the papers." Suddenly she felt inspired. "Monsieur, you are a man of means, are you not?"

Victor smiled. "I have been called that. Why?"

"I am not certain what these things might bring in sale, but would it be possible that you could purchase them, perhaps for your sister?" She held up her grandmother's things. "They are mine, so fear not that I have stolen them from the family coffers. My grandmother left them to me upon her death."

Victor took the combs and brooch and held them up against the firelight. "They are quite fine. The combs are ivory, and they look to be trimmed in gold and rubies."

"Aye. It was a gift from my grandfather who was well-propertied and in good stead with the king."

"And this brooch is of course quite valuable," Victor admitted.

"My grandmother said it was nearly one hundred years old. The gems are sapphires and rubies. I had thought to offer it to my father some time back, but I knew he'd never hear of it. Oh, monsieur, take pity on me now. Could you please find it in your heart to purchase these and give my father the money that he might pay off Monsieur Colbert?"

Victor considered the brooch for another moment before his hand closed around it. "Consider it done."

Jeanine let out a heavy sigh. "You are most kind. I will not forget you." If only he knew the degree to which that was true. She would forever remember his ruggedly handsome face, the long noble nose and thick black brows. She would ever think on the full lips and dark eyes that haunted her dreams.

With that much settled, Jeanine got to her feet and took up the shawl. "I am sorry I woke you, but not sorry that you have shared this time with me. It has comforted me greatly to know that at least one soul in this world knows the truth."

"But what of the truth?" Victor questioned. "Is there no one else to defend you in this matter? What of the time you spent away from your father's house?"

Jeanine smiled and shook her head. "It is of no importance now." She thought of Simon and his fierce defense of her. " 'Tis enough that you know."

"But where will you go?"

"I have some friends in the country," she said, suddenly realizing that this could well be her answer. She remembered the poor family who had arrived in Bruges not long ago with a severe intestinal disorder. They were en route to the home of the woman's parents and had assured her, upon their recovery and departure from Bruges, that should she ever need anything she had only to come to them. She knew roughly the area to which they had departed and now it seemed a logical choice.

"But how will you—"

Jeanine held out her hand to stop his questions. "It is unimportant, and if you knew where I was to go, you would have to tell them truthfully when they asked. I cannot have them following after me to force my hand. I pray you understand."

Victor got to his feet. "I do, but I cannot help but worry after your welfare."

"I go with God," she replied. "For once, with a clear conscience that no more lies will come between us."

She turned to leave, but Victor's warm hand closed over her arm. "At least let me offer you this," he said, handing her a small dagger. "There is great harm in the country— wild animals, highwaymen. Take this for protection."

Jeanine felt deeply touched that he should so worry about her. "Thank you. Your sister is a most fortunate woman." For a moment, Jeanine was perilously close to admitting her love for Victor. Looking into his dark, sympathetic eyes, she could almost believe he might return her feelings.

But just as she thought she might lose control, Victor broke the spell by sitting back down. He clutched at his side and offered her a lopsided smile. "I am impatient to be made whole."

Jeanine nodded, then without thought she offered a blessing. The same blessing she had murmured over him as Dr. Font. "May the Lord God heal you now. May He see your needs and reach where human hands may not go."

Victor's expression changed to one of perplexity. It was

as if he remembered her words from long ago. Jeanine held her breath and swallowed back the urge to explain. She turned instead and hurried to the door. "Please do not forget your promise to see to my father. I could not go in peace if I knew he would suffer even more."

Victor, lost in contemplation of a memory that would not come, nodded. "He will suffer the loss whether I give him money to settle his debt or not. He will suffer from your absence, but rest assured, I will see to your wishes. I owe this family my life, and on it, I pledge to see the matter taken care of."

Jeanine nodded and slipped from the room. She picked up the bag and placed the dagger inside, again touched by Victor's gesture. She stared longingly for a moment at the closed doors of her parents' and brother's rooms. Picking up the candle, she whispered her good-byes and made her way down to the first floor. Glancing around, she tried to imagine a life without the familiarity of all she had known the past twenty years. Every nook, every scratch and mark upon the wall suddenly seemed precious. Blowing out the candle, she sighed again. She couldn't look back, she told herself. Elsewise, she might never find the courage to go forward.

Pulling her cloak on, Jeanine closed the shop door and made her way around the side of the house. She had barely gone ten steps when a thick hairy arm closed around her neck. Screaming loudly, Jeanine remembered little else as the pressure increased and cut off her air supply.

nine

Victor had just managed to ease himself back into bed
when a scream that could only belong to Jeanine rent the
silence of the night. With strength he didn't know himself
capable of, Victor flew to the window and tried to make
out the images in the street below. Between the clouded
window and the dim light of the half-moon, Victor could
only see two nondescript figures scuffling in the street at
the edge of the property.

Jeanine!

It had to be her, and furthermore, it had to be Colbert or
one of his men. Victor made his way down the stairs, the
jostling giving him new degrees of pain. He knew he was
much recovered, but the nagging soreness from his leg
wounds coupled with the dull ache from his head and
chest made him very much aware that he was in no condition to fight for the honor of any woman.

He finally made the last step and crossed the darkened
shop of the first floor to open the outer door and peer into
the now empty street. Surely he hadn't imagined the
whole thing. He stepped out and looked up and down the
street, hoping for some indication of where the girl might
have gotten off to. But there was nothing. For a moment,
Victor even questioned whether their entire conversation
had been a dream. Then, as if to confirm the events of the
night, Victor spied Jeanine's bag.

He walked cautiously to the place where the bag had
been discarded, and with an eye turned ever upward to the
street around him, he bent to retrieve the article. Still there

was no sound or sight of Jeanine. Feeling exhaustion wash over him, Victor made his way back into the house. He would have to wake up one of the family, and because he knew Étienne better than the others, it would fall to Jeanine's brother to make the decision on what was to be done.

Dragging himself back up the stairs, Victor recalled the frightened expression on Jeanine's face as she had struggled to explain her situation. She had taken on the humiliation Colbert had placed upon her, and for what? What was it that caused her to allow everyone to believe such a lie about her? Clearly, it had caused her much pain and grief, or she'd never have found the need to explain herself to a complete stranger.

Knocking lightly upon Étienne's door, Victor was surprised at how quickly the thing was opened. It was almost as if Étienne had awaited his approach.

"Victor? What is it?"

"I fear I've come with bad news. Might you hear me out?"

"But, of course," Étienne said, sweeping a hand to motion Victor into his room. "Please sit. Even by my fire's light I can see you are quite spent."

"Thank you." Victor took a seat on the crude boot stool at the end of Étienne's bed. "I'm afraid Jeanine has gone. In fact, has been taken."

"What?"

Victor drew a deep breath, relieved that the pain had lessened in his chest. "She came to my room a few moments ago in order to retrieve some of her things."

Étienne frowned. "I am sorry she disturbed your rest."

"Not at all," Victor said, taking in the look of disgust upon the man's face. "Monsieur, I know we have little between us to call us friends, but I would like to be that to you and your family."

Étienne's expression changed to one of acceptance. "I find that most agreeable. Would that better circumstances might have thrown us together."

"Indeed," Victor said, then hurried to continue. "Your sister is innocent of the things which Colbert accused her of. I know this because she confessed it to me but a few moments ago."

"Confessed what?"

"She has never lain with Colbert. She despises the man, but there is some power over her which he has maintained in order to gain her compliance with his wishes."

"I had wondered at such a thing myself," Étienne admitted. "I saw him whisper to her on the streets, and while she nodded her agreement, she looked most disturbed at such tidings. Still, when she did not defend herself to our father, I assumed the worst."

"Aye, and we can only imagine why. The man is a brute and a beast as far as I can see. He has nothing to offer."

"Nothing, but the cancellation of our debt." Étienne's hand brushed back a wayward lock of hair. "Forgive me. I should not have made mention of that. 'Tis a family matter and naught for you to consider."

"But the matter has been given over to my consideration this very night. Your sister, indeed, has already bargained for the solution."

"She is the solution. Father saw no other way but to allow Colbert his request, nay, his demand that she marry him. Father would rather have rotted in debtor's prison than to allow Jeanine to become Colbert's wife had it only been himself that needed considering. But my mother's health is poor, and she would never have survived the conflict."

Victor nodded. "Jeanine knew this and knew too that by

running away she would only bring Colbert's punishment down upon her family. She knew he would call the debt due in full, which is why she made a request of me."

Étienne seemed not to hear him. "She actually ran away? I cannot believe she would put Father in this position."

Victor wanted to explain about the brooch and combs, but he knew that precious time was slipping away from them. "She didn't have a chance to run far," he interjected. "I heard a scream, and saw two people struggling in the street below. It was impossible to see who it was, but I'm certain Colbert probably staked men around the house fearing that Jeanine would run, as she did indeed decide to do."

"Colbert has taken her?" Étienne began, yanking on his clothes. "The man should be horsewhipped for the things he's done to her already."

Victor nodded. "She is innocent of any wrongdoing, of this I am certain. There is no telling what lies have been told in the past, and for what reason, but I feel confident that the words given me by your sister this night were true." The memory of her blessing came back to haunt him. He knew beyond a doubt that he'd heard the words given before, but he couldn't clearly remember where or when they'd been said.

Étienne pulled on his boots and stood. "I should wake up our father and see what is to be done."

"Please, before you do, let me say this. I owe you my life—indeed I owe your entire family my life and well-being. Let me return the service by arranging with Colbert to see this debt cleared. I am a man of means, and besides that, your sister—"

"No, monsieur," Étienne said, refusing to hear Victor out. "My father is a proud man. He would not hear of it. The kindnesses we have offered have been out of true Christian charity. Our Lord God admonishes us to care for one another as He has cared for us. Have you not heard the priest say that the Scriptures tell us if a man asks for your coat, give him your cloak also?"

"I have heard those words spoken," Victor replied, "which gives me standards for my desire to help you in return. Though I am not a strong man of God, I do desire to do right in the eyes of our heavenly Father. I may yet be the world's most terrible sinner, but I would seek to bless this family by whatever means are available to me."

Étienne smiled. "You have no need to pay a debt which is not rightly yours."

"And neither did our Savior, yet He bore our sins to a cross and died for us there that we might have eternal life."

"You are a difficult man," Étienne said, his grin even broader.

"I have been called that and more," Victor declared, matching the younger man's smile. "Now will you take me to Colbert that I might attempt to see this thing resolved?"

"But what of your injuries, man? You can barely sit a chair, much less a horse."

"I will manage," Victor promised. "I'm made of stronger stuff than you give me credit for. See now?" he asked, pulling back his dark hair. "Even now the wound on my head heals quickly. My ribs, though sorely abused, are not incapable of keeping me upright, and the wounds on my legs are still nicely bound in the bandages created by your dear mother. I lack only a steed and the direction of the man I seek. Will you be my guide?"

Étienne considered the matter for a moment. "It is nearly dawn. A visit to the estate of Colbert would not be out of line. Especially given that you are certain he has my sister within his walls."

Victor smiled. "Good. Then let us be at it." He continued

smiling even as he forced himself to stand. *Dear God,* he prayed, *give me the strength of which I boast, that I might help save this poor woman from her fate.*

"You dress, and I'll go ready the horses," Étienne suggested. "We have several miles to cover, so dress warmly."

Victor nodded. "What of your father and mother?"

"I'm fairly certain Father will hear the commotion and be up and about before we leave, but if not, I'll explain it later. Right now, Jeanine needs us."

"Yes," Victor said, a warmth spreading through his body like a flame. For all his reasoning, he could not set aside the desire to protect her.

❧

Jeanine could not see the face of her assailant, but in her heart she knew that the man was most likely a flunky of Colbert's. Having mercifully lost consciousness when assaulted, Jeanine had not awakened again until the rhythmic pounding of the horse's hooves against the roadway had jarred her senses. She tried to turn to see the man, but he roughly forced her back against him as his arm tightened its already painful hold on her. She slammed back against the thick, barrellike chest and struggled only briefly before the man threatened her.

"Settle yourself, or I'll see you bound and gagged and thrown over the back of this beast."

She stopped fighting, realizing the futility of her struggles, and instead took careful consideration of her surroundings. Light was just beginning to touch the distant horizon, and the sky was ever so gradually putting aside its blackness in favor of a rich indigo hue. Except for soreness in her throat and the man at her back, Jeanine might have enjoyed such a setting. But there was no enjoyment to be found in this perilous ride.

The horse continued at a full gallop for many miles

until the man finally slowed him to a trot. They were well away from the town proper, and Jeanine had little doubt that the estate which loomed up at them in the distance was none other than the home of Monsieur Antoine Colbert. She grimaced and tried not to think of what he would do to her. He would of course be furious that she had attempted to run away, but he had also obviously known she would try such a thing or he'd never have kept a man at her father's house.

Then again, what if this man was not paid by Colbert? *But of course, he must be,* she reasoned with herself. *Who else would care whether I came or went?*

"Where are you taking me?" she finally decided to ask.

"There," the man replied.

Jeanine thought to ask him to explain, but she decided against it. The man had been brutal enough, and her throat still ached from the stranglehold he'd put on her. If indeed Antoine Colbert awaited her, she would simply explain that Victor now had the money to pay off her father's debt and suggest he call upon the man before the ceremony of marriage be further considered. She was certain that money would mean more to him than a wedding to her. After all, the church insisted that both parties consent to marriage, and no worthy priest would consider performing a ceremony without her approval.

Still, Colbert had ways to hurt her that Jeanine hesitated to think about. There was Simon, but of course, for all she knew, he might be dead. She had hoped to see him before she'd left Bruges. She longed to know his state of health, and now that she had no choice but to go with her kidnapper and face whatever fate awaited her, Jeanine felt more desperate than ever to assure herself that Simon lived.

They rode through an open gateway and past stone walls that appeared to be the dividing defense of the land. Jeanine could see more clearly now as the molten orange of the sun cleared the newly grassed meadowland. Spring had come upon them without her notice. The countryside smelled of freshness and the promise of things to come. The man behind her was not quite so sweet of scent. He smelled as though he made his bed in the stables, and if he worked for Colbert, it probably was exactly where he slept.

The man reined back on the horse and halted at the heavy stone stairs that led upward to the front door of the estate. There were two towers on either side of the huge manor house that gave it the appearance of having tried hard to look like a castle fortress. While the building was of native stone and designed in the most modern architectural styling, it looked like nothing more than a prison to Jeanine. In her heart, she knew that was exactly what the estate would be for her.

Her captor forced her from the horse and, after binding her hands tightly behind her, dragged her up the stairs and into the house. She was surprised that no one came to greet them. She was especially surprised to find Colbert absent when she arrived at what was obviously the great common hall of the house.

"Here," the man said, shoving her to the right. "Up those stairs."

The open doorway revealed a spiral of stone steps that led up into an impenetrable darkness. "But we need a light," Jeanine protested. "I cannot see."

The man grunted and pushed her against the steps. Having no way to catch herself, Jeanine turned just in time to bear the weight of her fall on her left shoulder and hip. She struggled to regain a sitting position while the man apparently went after a torch. He returned just as she managed to steady herself against the tower wall and was contemplating how she might make her escape.

"Does this light make your ladyship happy?" The man's sarcastic tone and grimacing face left little doubt in Jeanine's mind that he cared nothing for her well-being. He was taller than her by a foot and appeared to be a giant of a man—thickly muscled and quite powerful. His nose, strangely bent to one side, suggested he'd seen more than one good fight in his lifetime, and that thought coupled with the fact that the man stood leering at her in a most distasteful manner caused Jeanine to become quite docile. She couldn't very well fight this man. Especially not bound as she was.

"Thank you," she forced herself to say, just before he yanked her to her feet with one of his beefy hands.

"Go on," he ordered.

They trudged up the stairs, Jeanine stumbling on the hem of her gown more than once. Each time the man seemed quite happy to put a hand on her. He laughed menacingly as she struggled to push him away, and Jeanine knew it was no use to further irritate him. Who knew what the man might do to her? Mayhap Colbert had even given the man free hand with her. She cringed at this thought and was about to offer up a prayer for safety when the stairway opened upon a room and the man shoved her inside.

She fell, this time face forward onto a cot. Grateful for the small amount of cushioning afforded her by the straw mattress, Jeanine hurried to turn and face her captor, but he'd have none of that. Putting his knee to the small of her back, he pushed her down.

"Stay there while I untie you," he ordered.

Jeanine swallowed hard, wishing silently that she might have a cup of water to quench her parched and aching throat. She felt tears welling up, and the fight to keep them from spilling over only made her throat feel worse.

"There," the man said.

Before Jeanine could turn over, the door to the room was pulled shut. Sitting up quickly, Jeanine realized that she was alone. There was the sound of a bar being lowered across the door outside, and she had little doubt that he'd just locked her into the room. It didn't matter. She was greatly relieved, at least momentarily, that he had gone and left her alone.

Spying a narrow slit of a window, Jeanine rushed over to stare outside at the lighted landscape. She was grateful for the cool air that rushed in against her face. Pressing her cheek against the smooth stone wall, she sighed and struggled to steady her nerves.

"Oh, Father God," she prayed aloud. "What is to become of me now? Will Antoine have his way? Am I to become his unwilling bride?" She let loose hot tears and sobbed into the sleeve of her houppeland. "Where are You, God? Am I to be as Job, stripped of all that I care for? Left to suffer alone?"

But she wasn't alone, she reminded herself, and neither had Job been. God was with her now, even as He had always been. Her actions had caused this thing to happen. She had no one to blame but herself. Sinking to the floor, she cried in earnest.

ten

Jeanine heard the door bar being lifted and knew that the time to confront her captor had come. She had not yet been told that this was the estate of Antoine Colbert, but she was certain that it could be no other. Trembling, she awaited the same lumbering giant who had taken her there the night before. The man motioned from the doorway, almost as if hesitant to come too close to her. He refused to smile or even acknowledge her with more than the single grunt and motion of his hand that indicated she should come with him.

Jeanine drew a deep breath and prayed for strength to face whatever came. She knew that only the hand of God would deliver her from a despairing fate. Step by step, she retraced her way to the ground floor, and when she emerged and came into the great room, she could see that Antoine Colbert did indeed await her.

"So you thought to escape our plans, eh?" he asked her and motioned her to take a seat at the table where food had been placed in order to break the fast. "We will eat and talk of this matter while my man goes to fetch the priest."

Jeanine shook her head, even though her stomach growled loudly in protest. "I will not share a table nor any other thing—be it name or bed—with you."

Colbert laughed. "If you choose not to eat then you punish only yourself. If you choose to refuse me, then it will be up to my own cunning to persuade you otherwise."

"I do not love you, Monsieur Colbert," Jeanine stated

frankly and came to the place where he now seated himself behind a huge platter of food. "I cannot marry a man for whom I have little regard, much less love."

"It takes not love, nor regard, to impregnate a woman," Colbert said crudely. "I need sons, woman! Not romantic platitudes and flowery words."

"Therein lies the difference between us, sir," Jeanine said, tilting her chin upward in defiance. "I require love. I cannot give myself in marriage to a man I despise."

"What? The good little Christian admits to despising her fellowman."

Jeanine felt her defenses go up like dry kindling to a spark. "I despise what you stand for, sir. I despise that you treat people like so much trash to be swept away. I despise that you have wronged and grieved my family."

"Wait there, wench. 'Twas not I who broke with our agreement," Colbert said, roast duckling midway to his mouth. He waved the drumstick like a scepter. "You were the one running away. You take up offense for the purported wrongs done you and your family, yet you lied to those very people in order to take yourself to the docks to play physician to the poor. Yea, and you lied to them as well, for they thought their good doctor was a man, not a scrap of a young woman."

Jeanine had no argument for him. She was guilty as charged and would have succeeded at her plans had Colbert not had the foresight to stop her. "I might once have been guilty of deception. That much I cannot deny. But those days are over. I have made a pledge to God that I will not lie. That is why, even for the sake of my family, I will not lie to God or the priest and make a pledge to you."

"We will be married, whether you lie or not," he said, finding her declaration of little interest.

"You are ruining the lives of good, gentle people, and

that does not bode well with me. My mother is heartsick. My father is filled with desperation. How can it be that you can find such joy in their defeat?"

"Because I am who I am. You can make all your pretty speeches about despising my actions and not me, but the truth is, my dear lady, my actions are a representation of who I am. I am heartless and bold. I am aggressive and self-centered, and I care not one whit what you think of me in that matter. I see you as a woman of health and ability. I see you as the vessel to carry my children and to nurture them when they are come to this earth. I do not need your love or admiration or even your honesty, but by my word, I will have your obedience and fear."

"So I am to be nothing more than your trained dog, monsieur?

Colbert laughed and tore off a chunk of the meat with his yellowed teeth. Grease ran down his beard. Speaking with his mouth full, he said, "Would that you might be as obedient as my hounds. You will come to understand your place in time, but for now sit and await the priest. Eat or eat not. It matters little to me."

Jeanine watched him as he shoved more food into his mouth and washed it down with who knew what from a silver goblet. She wanted to protest the game being played out between them, but silently went to the seat he had indicated her to take and waited what he would say. But before Colbert could clear his mouth, a servant appeared at the table.

"Sir, there have come visitors."

"Visitors? Here?" Colbert asked indignantly. "When no man was bid?" He seemed not to remember the open practice of offering hospitality to passing pilgrims.

"Aye, milord. Two men, but neither will speak to me their name."

Colbert considered this news for a moment, then waved the drumstick again in the air. "Bring them in, and we shall see what it is they are about."

The servant bowed briefly and hurried from the room. Jeanine could tell by the look on the smaller man's face that he'd been most grateful to have reason to leave. *No doubt he, too, had been witness to Colbert's temper,* Jeanine thought.

"So you are to have visitors for your wedding day," Colbert said by way of conversation.

"I have already told you, I cannot marry you. I do not love you, and I have already arranged for my father's debt to be paid." Jeanine suddenly regained her strength and continued in a hurried fashion before the strangers could appear. "You have but to consult Monsieur Pindar who is even now in residence in my father's house. He has the money to pay the debt and annul the contract."

Colbert laughed. "But I have no desire to annul any contract, and thus it remains legally binding. You are very foolish to think that this is an issue of money alone."

"But you said—"

"I said nothing that would indicate that I offered this contract solely based on your father's hefty debt. True enough, he owed me, but I've already made clear my first concern."

Jeanine shuddered. "An heir?"

"Aye," the man replied and speared a huge piece of pickled fish. Slopping the fish across the table to his platter, Colbert appeared to have lost interest in all else but food.

"Good morning, monsieur," Étienne called out as he and Victor entered the room.

Jeanine felt a surge of elation and relief course through her at the sight of them. *Thank You, heavenly Father*, she prayed silently and awaited her brother's demands that she be returned to the house of de la Fontaine.

"Ah, Monsieur de la Fontaine," Colbert replied. "Have you come to watch your sister take her vows in marriage?"

"No, I have come to put an end to such a farce. 'Twould hardly be fitting, given that she bears no child of yours and has never encouraged that such a union take place."

"So she told you of my little deception, eh? Well, 'tis of no matter. I intend to marry her this day or see your father thrown in debtor's prison along with his beloved wife. Oh, and of course you would join them now that you are partners with your father."

"And if I tell you that I have come to settle the debt?" Étienne questioned.

Jeanine's heart surged with hope. She got up from her chair and would have crossed to Étienne and Victor, but Colbert denied her such action.

"Sit!" he demanded, then motioned to two of his men who had lounged quietly in the shadows of the hall. "My men will help you back to your chair if need be."

"I do protest," Jeanine declared. "I have already told you that I will not marry you this day. You cannot keep me prisoner here."

"Oh, can't I?" Colbert asked, pushing back from his seat. He nodded toward her brother and Victor. "They are little match for my men. Do you doubt that I could see them both killed for trespassing before the sun crosses the sky?"

Jeanine felt herself grow lightheaded. "You would kill innocent men because I do not love you?"

"I would kill any man who stands in the way of that which belongs to me."

"She does not belong to you, Colbert," Victor stated matter-of-factly.

"Oh, and you believe she belongs to you?" Colbert asked.

Jeanine lowered her gaze to keep from betraying her feelings, but it was too late. She heard Colbert laugh menacingly.

"I have come to pay the debt owed by the family of François de la Fontaine," Victor announced, ignoring Colbert's comments.

Jeanine's head snapped up to meet Victor's gaze. He had come to her rescue. He had heard her screams and had known that Colbert was responsible for her disappearance, and he had come for her.

"I will not negotiate the terms with you, monsieur. You are not of the family."

"No, but I am a friend, and I owe this man my life."

" 'Tis of no concern to me. Surely you can understand that a man in my position has need of an heir. I desire this woman bear that heir, and because I own her father's notes, she will do as she is told."

"Will you also demand her firstborn be a son?" Victor asked sarcastically.

Jeanine could see that he was in pain. She could read it in his expression and wanted only to go to him.

"I will demand what I will, and you will have no part in it."

Victor shrugged. "I'm willing to double whatever is owed on the contract."

Jeanine gasped, her hand going to her throat where she clutched the fine linen of her gown. Her heart overflowed with love for Victor. Not only had he risked his life for her, but he was willing to give over his funds for her rescue. What more could she have desired of him, save love?

"Double, you say?" Colbert dropped the meat in his hand and stared at Victor for a moment, then turned his attention to Jeanine. "You would pay double to prevent our marriage?"

"As I said, I owe this man my life. His family has been good to see to my care, and I feel I must return the kindness."

"It must also help that she is obviously in love with you," Colbert said flatly.

Jeanine turned sharply to meet Colbert's intense gaze. The moment she saw his eyes, she knew that it would be impossible to deny the truth. However he had figured out her heart on the matter, Colbert would now use her feelings to destroy her. Suddenly she felt very afraid for Victor. What if Colbert decided to challenge him to some kind of duel? What if he called his men to simply throw Victor into the dungeon or the tower?

"You are merely trying to devise a means by which you can drive up your price," Étienne protested. "Your plan is foolishness. My sister barely knows this man. Now be reasonable and listen to what we propose."

"No, I believe I have found something far more interesting to focus on," Colbert said, getting to his feet. He wiped his greasy fingers on his coat and walked in a contemplative fashion toward Jeanine. He had grasped his pudgy hands together behind his back and was even now staring up at the ceiling as if to learn something important from the timbers there. Coming to stand in front of Jeanine, he paused and lowered his gaze. "You have declared this day that you do not love me. Perhaps you would care to enlighten this group as to whom you do love?"

Jeanine felt her face flush with heat. Her knees began to shake, and where Colbert had found it impossible to intimidate her before, now faced with having to admit her love for Victor, Jeanine thought she might actually faint.

"Well, my dear?" Colbert asked, pressing closer. "Care to offer up some of those romantic platitudes we discussed only moments before your brother's arrival?"

"Leave her be, Colbert," Étienne announced, coming forward to where they stood. Victor came along behind him as if uncertain what might next take place. Jeanine found it impossible to look either one of them in the eye.

"Your sister has proven in the recent past to be capable of deceit. She has, but this morning, declared herself to be finished with lies. She has made a pledge before God," Colbert said in a sardonic manner. He walked a pace or two away, then turned to eye Jeanine again. "So you understand, she has given her word to the God of heaven and earth, and to lie now would mean certainly that her soul would be forever condemned."

"What are you getting at, Colbert?" Étienne questioned.

Jeanine had begun to get a sick feeling in her stomach. Her instincts told her exactly what Colbert's motives were in this line of discussion. He intended to see her humiliated before Victor and her brother, and he didn't care at what price it came.

"Good sirs," he said, turning to Étienne and Victor. "I would very graciously consider your proposal of doubling my payment, on one condition."

Étienne looked at Victor quizzically before answering. "What is the condition?"

Colbert threw a look of wicked delight at Jeanine. His smug assurance was more than she could bear. She knew without him speaking the words that he would ask her to bare her heart before them now.

"If your sister can deny that she holds love for this man, then I will accept your payment and cancel the contract of marriage."

All eyes turned to Jeanine. She swallowed hard and lowered her head. "But of course, I love all mankind," she said, barely above a whisper.

"Ah, but that is not what I speak of," Colbert replied.

"For I see even now a spark of passion between you and Monsieur Pindar."

"This is utterly ridiculous," Étienne said, shifting uncomfortably.

"Is it? If that be the case then I will be a wealthy man, *non?*" Colbert took hold of Jeanine's arm. "Tell then true, my dear. Do you or do you not fancy yourself in love with this man? Remember now, you have vowed to God from this day forward nevermore to lie."

The silence was unbearable. Jeanine lifted her face to meet Victor's confused expression. Her brother seemed annoyed and anxious to be done with the entire matter, but by the look on Victor's face, Jeanine could tell that even now he was coming to understand that Colbert's suggestion was not totally unfounded.

Oh, Father, Jeanine prayed, *how can I admit to this thing without totally humiliating myself?* She took a deep breath.

"Well, milady?" Colbert pressed.

Jeanine nodded. *"Oui,"* she said with heavy resignation. "I love him."

Étienne stopped shifting and stared at her in dumfounded silence. Jeanine couldn't even bring herself to look at Victor. She couldn't bear it if she found abhorrence or disgust in his expression.

"So, there you have it gentleman. My betrothed has fallen in love with another and has been unfaithful to our contract. I could have her put away, perhaps even stoned for adultery."

"I have done nothing wrong, monsieur!" Jeanine declared, no longer caring about her bruised emotions. "I have never played you false. I have never loved you, nor have I approved of this arrangement. I only agreed for the sake of my father's debt, but now it can be paid otherwise, and you have no right to force me into a loveless marriage."

Colbert laughed menacingly. "You are very wrong, milady. I have full right to you and to our marriage. But it grieves me to know that you are in love with this man. Mayhap I should call him out, here and now, and be done with it. 'Tis unseemly that I should go forward into our marriage with another man sharing love with my wife."

"He doesn't feel anything for me," Jeanine protested. "The feelings are all on my part."

"I find that impossible to believe." Colbert turned on the stunned men. "After all, he is here offering his funds to save you from my clutches."

Jeanine opened her mouth to offer some weak argument but was saved from further disgrace when Colbert's servant appeared.

"Sir," the man said nervously, "the priest has come."

eleven

"By all means, send him in," Colbert said, wiping his hands against his rotund belly. The cotehardie he wore was of crimson velvet and did nothing to hide the stains.

Jeanine fled his presence and threw herself into her brother's arms. "You cannot let him do this. I swear I'll throw myself off the tower before becoming his wife."

Étienne wrapped a protective arm around her shoulder. "You heard her, Colbert. She prefers death to sharing your name."

"I'll put a guard on her, rest assured. Your precious sister will not meet with any untimely fate."

Jeanine searched her brother's face, praying to find an answer in the depths of his eyes—finding nothing there but hopelessness and anger. She fell silent as the priest came into the room. His pious nod was the only acknowledgment he gave her.

To her surprise, before either Colbert or the priest could speak, Victor posed a question. "Good father, is it not the wishes of the church to see both parties agreeable in the marriage union?"

The priest turned and nodded. "But of course. Marriage is ordained by God as a most holy union. Both man and woman must agree to the arrangement."

Victor smiled smugly at Colbert. Jeanine watched him issue a silent challenge and felt hope surge within her. Clutching Étienne's hand, she turned to face the priest.

"I must beg your pardon then, Father," she said without hesitation. "I do not wish to marry."

The priest shook his head and turned to Colbert. "Are you the one who has sent for me this day?"

"I am," Colbert responded, his eyes black with hate.

"And were you aware that the woman was not in agreement with marriage?"

"I was and am even now aware," Colbert admitted. Then to Jeanine's utter surprise, he added, "But 'tis hardly a wedding I am suggesting between myself and this witch."

"What say you, man?" Étienne growled out the question. He put Jeanine aside and stepped forward as if challenged. "You had better explain yourself."

"You both heard me," Colbert replied.

Jeanine cast a helpless look at the priest, then without thinking, turned to look into Victor's dark eyes. He seemed to consider her for a moment, then smiled ever so slightly, leaving Jeanine's heart aflutter. Would the circumstance have been different, she might have offered an explanation and declared that her love for him was pure and true, but instead she found Colbert's enraged voice interrupting her thoughts.

"See, even now she is trying to cast her spells upon this good man."

"I am doing nothing of the kind," Jeanine responded in anger. "I am no witch, and I protest your accusations."

"Sir, by what means do you accuse this young woman?" the priest questioned quite seriously.

"I have witnessed her actions myself," Colbert replied. "Ask her yourself. Ask her to deny that she has concocted potions for the purpose of producing effects on the bodies of her victims."

The priest turned. "What say you of this?"

"He has twisted the truth, milord." She looked to her brother for support, but Étienne and Victor both looked at her with questioning expressions.

"Mayhap we might sit," said the priest. "My journey here was much hurried and tiresome."

"Oh, but of course," Colbert said, the picture of congeniality. "We were just breaking the fast, perhaps you would care to join in?"

"Nay," the priest declined. "I wish for this most heinous accusation to be addressed."

Colbert led them to a small solarium off the great hall and waited until all parties were seated before shutting the door with a loud thud. Jeanine jumped at the noise and felt all gazes once again settle on her.

The priest scrutinized her with his pale blue eyes, as if weighing by mere sight the value of Colbert's words. "Are you in the habit of practicing witchcraft?" he asked quite frankly.

"*Non,* Father. I am not." Jeanine glanced to where Colbert had seated himself.

"Monsieur, would you please explain your proof?"

Colbert passed a brief smile upon Jeanine before answering. "This woman was to be my wife. Her father signed the marriage contract with me some weeks past. It was my belief that she was pure of heart and godly in her practices. She was known to attend church and to honor her parents, and I believed her of good quality. However," he paused, looking first to Jeanine and then to Étienne and Victor, "there came a suggestion to me that my intended might be less than honorable."

"How so?" asked the priest.

"She was seen to be loitering about the docks. This happened not once, but many times, often on a daily basis."

"And what were her actions while upon the docks?"

Colbert sneered. "She did not stay upon the docks. She took herself to a book copy shop owned by a Jew named Simon Grosz."

Jeanine shifted uncomfortably and tried to concentrate on the dark blue linen of her gown. How could she explain to the priest that it was only her desire to heal the sick that sent her to Simon? No matter what she said, she'd be condemning herself in the eyes of the church. She had consorted with a Jew and practiced medicine. Not only that, she had performed surgery, and it was well-known that such things were widely opposed in the church. Jeanine scarcely thought of anything else, however, as Colbert launched into the matter of her love for Victor Pindar.

The priest raised his hand for Colbert's silence. "The things you have shared are in no way proofs to me of this woman's participation in the black arts. Have you something more compelling?"

Colbert nodded. "Indeed I have. The book copy shop Mademoiselle de la Fontaine frequented was only a cover for her practices. The old man, Monsieur Grosz, was nearly blind and could not possibly have operated a copy shop with any competency."

"And it was while here that you believe she was practicing witchcraft?"

"I know it to be. I followed her there and found that in her spell-casting she had taken on the form of a man. She was dressed completely in black and her hair had taken on the course, gray-black texture of the old Jew. Her face was blackened and she moved about the room preparing all manner of potion in preparation for her spells."

"Is this true?" the priest asked Jeanine.

"Father, the circumstances hold some basis of truth, but not in the manner for which Monsieur Colbert would have you believe. I was merely seeking to help Simon—Monsieur Grosz—"

"So you admit to consorting with the Jew?"

Jeanine felt a deep sense of frustration from his interruption. "Simon and I became friends. He did not seek to turn me from my faith in God."

The priest appeared quite vexed about this and looked to Colbert for help. "Can this Jew be summoned?"

"Nay," Colbert replied, eyeing Jeanine for her response. "He is dead. She killed him."

"Nay!" Jeanine declared, jumping to her feet. " 'Tis untrue!"

"She found me in the room and was greatly distressed. Her spell was broken, and I was able to see clearly that she was but a woman in men's clothing. I opposed her, and she argued with me most bitterly. She threatened my life, and when I laughed at her, she began to chant her incantations. The Jew got in the way, however, as he feared I might strike her away. When she threw the spell, it was the Jew and not myself who bore the effects."

The priest's eyes narrowed and his expression changed to one of obvious distaste. "And what were those effects?"

"He immediately clutched his chest and fell over dead. 'Twould have been my fate had the old man not got in the way."

"I see. And what say you for yourself, young woman?" the priest questioned coolly. Gone was any attempt at cordiality.

"I did not cast a spell. Simon's heart attacked him because he was worried about me. Monsieur Colbert was most unkind and treated me quite roughly. Simon was only attempting to protect me."

"No doubt he practiced her black art, as well," Colbert replied.

Throughout the entire interrogation, Jeanine had noted her brother's looks of confusion and disbelief, as well as Victor's seemingly intense study of each person in the room. She wanted to scream that they should all just go away and leave her to her humiliation, but it was not to be.

"Given the circumstances and the evidence," the priest said, getting to his feet, "it is my suggestion that the young woman be held where she cannot harm anyone else. Give her over to a room which has been blessed and strip it of all articles. Put nothing more than a pallet of straw upon the floor and a blanket to ward off the chill. Bring her meals on a flat board and give her nothing but water to drink."

Colbert nodded enthusiastically, but Étienne had finally reached his limit of silence. "Hold there, Father," he said, rising to meet the priest face-to-face. "This woman is my sister, and I have never known her to consort with demons or cast spells. She is well known in the community as a God-fearing soul, and she is generous with her time for those who need her."

"As much as I would like to believe you," the priest replied, "I have seen the likes before. Ofttimes we believe ourselves to have knowledge of a person, only to be astonished by their true natures."

"I will grant you that people are many times not who they appear to be, but this case is different."

The priest held up his hand. "We will save her defense for her trial before the council of the church."

"What!" Jeanine exclaimed. Now, she, too, was on her feet. "But I have done nothing."

"Nothing save kill a man," Colbert reminded his audience.

"You will be held here on the estate of Monsieur Colbert," the priest stated firmly. "I will arrange for the council, and your trial date will be set. Until that time you are to be held without any visitation from others lest you cast your spells upon them and seduce them to aid you in your circumstance."

"But I am innocent!" Jeanine felt herself growing ill at

the thought of weeks, mayhap even months under Colbert's heartless keep.

"That is for the church to decide," the priest replied without emotion. "Until that time, you will abide by this decree or face excommunication." He turned to Étienne and Victor. "That would also go for any man who aids her in an attempt to avoid trial."

Jeanine saw Victor's eyes darken and his jaw grow tense. She wondered if it was the pain of his ribs or anger which caused such reaction. She had little time to contemplate it, however, as Colbert motioned for his men to take Jeanine in hand.

"Remove her to the tower."

"First allow me to bless the room."

Colbert bowed to the priest. "But, of course. Come, I will lead the way while my men stand guard over the woman."

Colbert and the priest took their leave, and Jeanine found herself staring after them in disbelief. How could her life have become so completely topsy-turvy?

"Jeanine," Étienne whispered, reaching out to touch her arm. "I will find help. I will figure out what must be done."

Victor slowly stood, and Jeanine caught her breath as his expression warmed. "We will work together," he assured her.

She wanted very much to say something, anything that might ease the embarrassment of her declaration of love, but for the life of her there seemed nothing of sense to be told. If she tried to justify her feelings, it would only serve to dig her deeper into the grave she'd already prepared for herself. Tears formed in her eyes and streamed down her face. She tried hard to ignore Colbert's burly guards as Étienne took her into his arms and comforted her.

"Hush, sweet sister," he whispered. "All will be well. You will see."

"I see only the hopelessness of this situation. Oh, what have I done?"

"That, I suppose, is yet to be discovered. Tell me in truth, what cause did you have to go to the old man's shop every day?"

Jeanine choked back her sobs. "I was working as a doctor, nothing more—nothing less. Simon had trained me in the ways of medicine. I only wanted to help the poor. They have so little, and when they fall ill, they cannot afford the care of a physician. I only wanted to help them." Her body shook fiercely with sorrow.

"Jeanine?" Victor spoke her name soft and sweet.

Raising up from where she'd buried her face against Étienne's tunic, she met his sympathetic gaze. *"Oui?"*

"Do not despair. God is with you."

Jeanine sniffed back tears. "I am sorry to have made you a part of this." She wanted to ensure his freedom from further entanglements with her cause.

To her surprise, he grinned and raised her hand to his lips. "I have no regret of it. It gives me much to consider."

Jeanine lowered her gaze and fought the pounding of her heart. His lips were warm on her hand and the very thought that those lips might one day touch her own, caused her to momentarily forget her problems.

"Listen to me, Jeanine," Étienne said, breaking the spell. "We will go back to town and seek out help."

"Please, please find out what happened to Simon," she begged.

"Of course," Étienne promised. "He might well aid us in this case."

"I pray it is so, but only if he can be kept from harm. He is a Jew—that much is true. And he was practicing medicine illegally, just as I did. But he is no demonic soul. He believes in God, albeit, he rejects Christ as his Savior."

"I will find the old man and talk to him. Try to be strong. We have very little control over Colbert or the priest's actions. You will be cared for, but if Colbert so much as lays a finger on you, I will personally see to his death."

"As will I," Victor promised.

"Thank you, both," Jeanine said, just as Colbert and the priest reentered the room.

"It is completed," Colbert announced.

"I ask you, Father," Étienne commented, as Colbert took Jeanine in hand, "what protection does my sister have against this man's unwelcome advances?" Colbert reddened and his grip tightened on Jeanine's arm. Étienne continued, "She is a maid, innocent and pure, whether Colbert chooses to believe such or not. I have heard of this man's reputation, and I fear for my sister."

The priest looked from Étienne to Colbert and Jeanine. Then, as if seeing the man's concern as valid, he nodded. "Monsieur Colbert, I charge you in the name of the Father, Son, and Holy Spirit, that no harm either physical or spiritual might come upon this woman. She must be tried before the council. If she is a witch, it will be up to the church to determine her fate. If she is found innocent, then she must be allowed to return to her life, unharmed and unknowledgeable of the ways of the world. Will you assure me on threat of excommunication that you will see to this woman's safety?"

Colbert grimaced then forced a laugh. "I would not dream of touching the witch on fear of my soul."

The priest was satisfied, and Jeanine knew there was nothing else Étienne could demand. She caught one final glance from Victor and an assuring nod from her brother before being led from the room and back to the cold stone stairs of the tower.

"You thought to have victory over me," Colbert whispered in her ear as they ascended the steps together, "but 'tis I who have the victory."

"You are wrong, monsieur," Jeanine said, pausing long enough to meet Colbert's cold stare. "The victory will be God's and God's alone. He will not tolerate your lies against one of his own. I have learned my lesson about speaking the truth, but you have yet to learn yours."

twelve

Nearly a month had passed, with only the briefest of messages sent by Colbert to Jeanine's family. Learning the fate of their daughter, François and Margarite de la Fontaine had appealed to Colbert for mercy, but he had made it quite clear that the matter was out of his hands. They had paid a visit to the cathedral only to discover that their own priest was reluctant to interfere until the church formally resolved the conflict.

Étienne had gone back to the shop where Simon had cared for Victor, but the old man was gone and the shop was closed up tight. After asking neighboring establishments about the old man's whereabouts, Étienne was no better off. Simon had seemingly disappeared into thin air.

Victor found the waiting almost more vexing than anyone else, and for reasons that came as a total surprise to himself. As his wounds healed and he spent his time in recuperative rest, he couldn't stop thinking back to Jeanine's declaration of love. He always smiled as he remembered her embarrassment and shy regard for him. How odd that the maid had fallen in love with him.

As the days slipped by, Victor's contemplation led him to startling discoveries, and as he realized the full implication of his thoughts, he couldn't bring himself to believe his conclusion. Cornering Jeanine's brother late one night, he shared his theory.

" 'Twould seem you have much on your mind to keep you from rest," Étienne said, as Victor joined him in front of the common room fireplace.

"I would not wish to awaken your parents, but my thoughts are such that sleep is quite impossible," Victor responded in a hushed voice. "I've been thinking about Jeanine."

"Ah," Étienne replied and poked the fire. "Her words of love, I suppose."

Victor grinned. "Well, there is always that to turn my head. What of your sister's declaration? Have you ever known her to speak thusly?"

"You mean to declare herself in love?"

"Aye."

"Hmmm, let me think back. There was that one time when Pierre lived next door. He was dark-eyed, just as you are. Perhaps that is the attraction," Étienne teased.

"And she was in love with him?" Victor asked, not liking that such conversation made him feel tense.

"Oh, that she was. She was always after his attentions." Victor sat in glum silence, and Étienne roared with amusement. "Of course, she was only six at the time."

Victor caught the look of knowing on Étienne's face and shrugged. "I suppose it is hard to help myself from feeling something for her. She looked so forlorn standing there. To imagine Colbert having the nerve to accuse her of witchcraft."

"*Oui,* but she had gone to Simon's in order to illegally practice medicine."

"Which is truly where my thoughts are leading me this night," Victor admitted.

"How so?"

Victor hunched his shoulders and leaned his elbows on his knees. "Jeanine is the one who cared for me. She is most likely the one who performed the surgery on me."

Étienne looked at him in stunned silence. Victor knew

that his words were preposterous. It was hard enough to imagine that he had survived the ordeals of brain surgery, but to suggest that a slip of woman like Jeanine had taken the instruments in hand to complete the task was almost more than he could allow himself to believe.

"I know what you are thinking, because I've thought it myself," Victor admitted. "She is but a woman, petite and weak, but you yourself heard Colbert's evidence. He stated that Simon Grosz had such weak eyesight that he could not possibly perform the tasks of book copying. How much less would he be able to perform surgery?"

"I suppose you have a point worth noting," Étienne agreed. "But Jeanine?"

Victor laughed. "I can believe almost anything possible of that woman. She could not have surprised me more with her declaration of love. To tell me she saved my life as well seems most fitting."

"But surgery? To actually cut into a man's flesh and bone?"

Victor nodded. "And then to care for him in the guise of a male physician, all in order to see to my needs. 'Twould be then, most likely, that her feelings developed for me."

"For all the good it does either of you now," Étienne said, reminding Victor instantly of their plight.

"Aye, 'tis a difficult situation at best. I've given over long hours to prayer, but the answers seem slow in coming. I have one hope, besides my faith," Victor added.

"And what might that be?"

Victor eased back in the chair. "I have posted a letter to the king."

"You what?" Étienne's voice raised in surprise.

"I have overseen the creation of several buildings for the king. Two cathedrals and a summer estate, to name a few. I've held his favor for some time, as well as that of

England's king. I've sent a post to him, as well, through my sister."

"You could not surprise me more had you told me you'd journeyed to Rome to plead Jeanine's case before the pope," Étienne admitted.

"If I thought it would do any good, I'd gladly go there. I can't help but feel responsible for this situation. Perhaps if your sister hadn't fallen in love with me, she might have married Colbert without a fuss or fight."

"Then you do not know my sister very well," Étienne responded.

"No, but I'd like to," Victor said with a sad smile.

"Truly?" Étienne watched him carefully as if searching for some telltale sign that he lied.

"Truly. I have to admit, I came to enjoy her companionship while she cared for me. Now, just thinking of her stuck in that place with Colbert. . ." He fell silent, anger evident in his expression.

"What goes on here?" François de la Fontaine asked, coming sleepily into the room. "I thought I heard voices."

"*Oui,* and I'm sorry we woke you," Étienne said. "We were just discussing Jeanine."

"And what else would we talk about these days? I can scarce work for thinking of her. My poor, poor child." Monsieur de la Fontaine sat down heavily and put his head in his hands.

"I've come up with a plan to steal her away from Colbert," Victor said, surprising both father and son.

"You might as well not try," Étienne said, before his father could respond. "Colbert guards that place like a fortress. He will have her under bar and lock, no doubt. He has quite an army of men, and you must remember he owns most everything your eye can take in."

"I care naught for what he owns. I weary of awaiting the

church's decision of when they might come and listen to her case. I am angry that an entire moon has cycled itself in full while a young woman's life hangs in the balance."

Jeanine's father looked up and eyed Victor carefully. "You speak as one who cares."

"I do care. I care more than I had believed myself capable of. I feel responsible too, for it is of my opinion that much of this might never have happened if I had never entered your house."

"Hardly that!" his host exclaimed. "You have done nothing but attempt to rescue us from despair and certain doom. If you must fault anyone, fault me for signing the marriage contract. I felt foolishly that there was no other way. I did not trust God to provide, and this is my punishment."

"I think you're both wrong," Étienne replied. "This is evidence of Colbert's corruption. 'Tis nothing of our fault, either implied or imagined. Colbert is evil and heartless, and he has begun this thing—but I will see it finished."

"As will I," Victor promised.

"You mustn't try to take Jeanine from the tower," her father admonished. "The Lord, Himself, knows that if I thought it would work, I would try it, but we would need an army stronger than any I can imagine. No, we must appeal to the church council and pray God intervenes on Jeanine's behalf."

"It would be most helpful to find what became of Simon Grosz," Victor said, with a yawn. "I believe on the morrow I will go in search of him again. After all, it has been a fortnight since we talked to the dock folk. Mayhap someone has heard of something since our time there."

"I'll go with you, if you like," Étienne offered.

"*Non,* you have enough that demands your attention. I will search, and if I find something, I will consult you both."

In his room later that night, Victor was more than a little aware of Jeanine's presence. The bedroom had been hers for who knew how long, and even now the fresh scent of her lavender soap could sometimes be caught in the air.

Victor tried hard not to think of her fearful expression as Colbert led her away. Thinking about that scene made him want to go for a horse and journey posthaste to Colbert's estate. Growing frustration nagged at him, and in spite of the late hour, Victor wondered seriously if sleep would ever be his companion that night.

He went to the dresser where Jeanine had many of her concoctions and herbs. He smiled as he imagined her studying the effects of each and what their medicinal values might be. He picked up one bottle and tried to imagine what the leafy green object was inside. That was when he spied the slip of paper beneath the bottle. Picking it up, Victor opened it to find the words, *Five Geese Flying*. He noted the script was feathery and disjointed, as if the hand that held the quill had been feeble and shaky. Had Simon Grosz been the author of the message? If so, what did the message signify?

Tucking the slip of paper inside his tunic, Victor vowed that on the morrow he would find Simon, dead or alive. Victor would seek to set into motion the future of the young woman who so fearfully admitted her love for him.

Victor paused outside the ramshackle shop front that identified Simon Grosz's residence and book copy shop. Unlike two weeks earlier when the place had born no sign of life, today the door was very much open, as were the windows. Stepping up to the portal, Victor knocked loudly and announced himself.

"*Bonjour,* is anyone here?" Victor made the decision to

step inside and call again. *"Bonjour?"*

"Bonjour, monsieur," Simon said, coming slowly from the back room. "Ah, Monsieur Pindar, is it not?"

"Oui," Victor replied. " 'Tis I."

"I had thought perhaps we would not meet again," Simon replied. "Please, come inside and sit with me. How are you feeling?" The old man tottered a bit as he led the way to a small table where two chairs awaited their attention.

"I might ask the same of you. It was my understanding that you had fallen ill. As for myself, I am well. Thanks be to you, God, and Jeanine de la Fontaine."

"Do you know of her? How is she?" Simon's face was grief-stricken. "I have thought of her constantly and asked blessings on her. A horrible man, Antoine Colbert, took her from me some time back. I could not help her, and now I fear—"

"The news is not good. Colbert has accused her of witchcraft," Victor admitted.

"But I thought he wished to share matrimony with her."

"He did, but Mademoiselle Jeanine had other thoughts."

"I know that well," Simon replied, then lowered his face and smiled. "She did not have love for Monsieur Colbert. Her heart was otherwise engaged."

"Oui. I know it well."

"So she told you?"

Victor grinned. "It was not in the setting she would have liked, but yes. To my great shame, I must admit that Colbert ascertained her heart before I did."

"I suppose that did not brook well with the man," Simon said, the amusement in his voice quite evident.

"Non, it did not. I believe that is why he decided to accuse her of witchcraft. He had already sent for the priest to marry them, and when I pointed out, with the priest as witness, that the church required both parties to agree to

marriage, Colbert changed his story. He told the priest he no longer desired to marry Jeanine, but that he had sent for him to accuse her before the church of witchcraft. He cited the day he found her here posing as a doctor."

Simon looked surprised. "You know of her work?"

"*Oui.* I know, too, that she is the one responsible for this," he said and pulled back earth-black hair.

Simon leaned forward to take in the trephining scar. "It has healed well."

"She is the one who performed the surgery, is she not?"

Simon nodded. "I told her what to do, and she saved your life. Blood was pooling against the brain, and it left you unconscious. 'Twould have killed you had we not opened up your head and relieved the pressure."

Victor smiled. "She has gotten into my head in more than one way."

Simon chuckled. "Jeanine has a way of doing that. 'Tis certain the girl has a gift, and I only sought to help her use it. True, it is against our laws, and I have probably jeopardized her life by my foolishness. I only longed to pass on that which I knew and to help her realize her desires to help others."

"You did the right thing, Simon. Elsewise, I'd be long departed from this earth." Victor pulled the slip of paper from his tunic and handed it over to Simon. "I found this in her room last night. What meaning has it?"

Simon looked at the words and nodded. "*Five geese flying* was a code we agreed upon. It was my message for her to come to the docks for emergencies. Otherwise, she slipped down here whenever she could, and we would study and improve her knowledge."

"But why *five geese flying?*"

" 'Tis from Jeanine's own stories of childhood. Her grandmother was a storyteller, and before she died she had imparted many tales of spiritual value. Her grandmother told Jeanine of the geese and how five geese flew overhead the day she met Jeanine's grandfather. Five geese also were seen from her window the day she gave birth to Jeanine's father. She believed it a sign of hope and love. It seemed fitting for the calling of a physician to aid in the healing of his, or her, in this case, beloved people."

Simon smiled as Victor tried to put all the pieces together. "But there were other reasons for the attachment to such matters," he continued.

"Jeanine's grandmother reminded her of how the geese would fly south in the autumn. With the winter and the burial of all that seemed alive, she would admonish Jeanine to search her heart and soul for that which should be left as dead. Hurtful feelings, ugly words said without thought, the kind of things that were best left buried with the coming winter snows."

Victor nodded his understanding, and Simon continued. "Then too, with the return of the geese and the coming of spring and summer, Jeanine was encouraged to open her heart to new growth. Her grandmother told her to seek out God's direction for her life and to know the renewing of the spirit that only He could give."

"Jeanine's grandmother sounds to be a very wise woman," Victor said softly.

"When she left this world," Simon added, "she left a deep void in Jeanine's heart." He shrugged. "But who knows, mayhap you will fill that void, eh?"

"Mayhap," Victor replied, deep in thought. "Mayhap. But first, we must find a way to free her from Colbert's plans. He would see her burned at the stake rather than give her over to me. I have tried to come up with a plan for her defense, but it seems that I am lacking direction in that area."

"Jeanine would say that the direction we seek is only

a prayer away."

Victor eyed the old man with a knowing nod. "*Oui,* she would say exactly that."

"Then we must honor her and listen to just that suggestion, *non?*"

"You are very right, my dear fellow. I allowed myself to grow discouraged and to take my eyes from the hope that I have in God. But no more. I will be in touch," Victor said, getting to his feet. "Please send word to me at Monsieur de la Fontaine's residence should you need me. The previously arranged code will work as well for me as it did Jeanine."

Simon laughed and followed Victor out of the shop. "Mayhap our little goose will do her own flying soon."

"I pray it will be so," Victor told the old man.

thirteen

Jeanine found herself brought before the church council and, to her surprise, a gathering board of university physicians. The two groups seemed to be unlikely companions, but for the purpose of stamping out witchcraft they appeared willing to tolerate each other. They were seated at a long table at the head of the great hall.

The physicians took up the left side of the table. They seemed almost bored and annoyed by the summons which had brought them to Flanders. On the right side of the table were the clergy. Two scribes, clerks to the bishop, sat side by side, and in the center sat the bishop himself. He was by far the most foreboding of the group. He stared at her stern-faced and dark-eyed, and his expression was one of complete intolerance.

Jeanine, herself, had been made to stand in the center of the room. She was allowed to bathe and wear a clean gown, which her mother had brought to her that morning, and her hair had been braided and a plain simple cap of white linen had been placed upon her head. She knew she must look ridiculously small before the mighty assembly of men, but she bit back her fear and bolstered her determination. She would face the truth nose to nose, and whether these men found value in her work or not, she would refuse to lie in order to ease her discomfort.

"We will now hear the case of Jeanine de la Fontaine," the bishop said, glancing down at the parchment in front of him.

Jeanine glanced around, comforted marginally by the

presence of her family, but deeply wounded by Victor's absence. She tried to offer her mother a smile, but found it impossible. She had only to look into the anguished faces of her parents for tears to form in her eyes. Étienne appeared stalwart and true, but his brow was wrinkled in worry. Jeanine turned back to face her accusers. It was infinitely easier to face her enemies than her loved ones. What did she care if she disappointed those folk who wished her nothing but ill? But to see the sorrow and fear in the eyes of her family was more than she could bear.

"Who accuses this woman of heresy and witchcraft?" the bishop asked impatiently.

Jeanine turned to meet the scowling gaze of Antoine Colbert. For the last month she had endured his advances and lewd suggestions, all the while reminding him of the priest's threat of excommunication. Colbert cared very little about the church and whether or not he found acceptance in the eyes of Rome, but he did care about his businesses and landholdings. He knew that to anger the church would mean certain financial doom.

"I accuse her," Colbert said, struggling against his rotund midsection to stand.

"Your name, sir?" the bishop asked by way of meeting the formalities. His clerks were busy dipping their quills and noting all details of the conversation.

"I am Antoine Colbert."

"Monsieur Colbert, do you hereby give charge in the sight of God and these witnesses that this woman, Jeanine de la Fontaine, did willingly participate and practice the black arts of witchcraft?"

"I do," Colbert replied solemnly.

The bishop conferred with the man at his left before continuing. "Mademoiselle de la Fontaine, you have heard the charges. How do you plead your case?"

Jeanine did not hesitate. "I am innocent."

The council murmured as the bishop made comment and waited while the clerks penned her response. He stared at Jeanine with a stoic expression, and for a moment, she had the distinct impression that he'd already decided that she was guilty as charged.

"Monsieur Colbert, are you prepared to offer evidence to this council and give proof to the practices of this woman?"

"I am, your Grace. I have witnessed her actions myself and come here this day to expose her schemes."

"I will hear your testimony now," the bishop announced and leaned back into his chair.

Colbert looked hard at Jeanine before continuing. "This woman was to have been my bride. Her father, Monsieur François de la Fontaine, may bear witness to this truth. The details were agreed upon, the contracts signed, and Mademoiselle de la Fontaine was known to be in preparation for our wedding." He paused as if to defy Jeanine to deny what he said.

"It was during this time of preparation that I learned of mademoiselle's journeys into a most undesirable part of our town. Daily she would venture down to the docks and disappear into the rundown shop of the Jew, Simon Grosz."

"And upon learning this, what did you do?" the bishop questioned.

"I feared for the lady's virtue and followed her inside. It was there that I found she had transformed herself into the appearance of a man."

The council, as well as the physicians, began muttering among themselves. The clerks wrote furiously and appeared not in the leastwise to concern themselves with the implications of what had been stated.

"She was transformed, you say," the bishop more stated

than questioned. "How so?"

Jeanine allowed her thoughts to drift to a place of protection and security. She pictured herself sitting at the feet of her *grandmère*. She could almost feel the old woman's gentle hand upon her head. *Oh, Grandmère,* she thought, *my lies have brought me to destruction. I stand accused of all manner of falsehood by a man who would see me dead because of my rejection of him as husband.* She could imagine her grandmother smiling upon her, bidding her to calm her fears and place her trust in God.

"And you saw her actually cast a spell in your presence?" the bishop now asked Colbert.

Jeanine turned to see his reaction. He narrowed his eyes at her, and there was little doubt in her mind that he would gladly spark the fire that would consume her life.

"She thought to kill me," Colbert replied. "She cast a spell, but God was with me. I moved aside and the Jew Simon Grosz received her vengeance instead."

"He lies!" Jeanine called out.

"Silence, woman. We will determine what falsehoods are spoken," the bishop told her. "Monsieur Colbert, what happened to the Jew?"

"He began clutching his chest, and it was evident that the pain he experienced was most grave. He collapsed to the floor at that point, and while the witch—I mean, mademoiselle—was distracted, I yanked off her disguise and broke the spell of transformation."

"I see. What became of the Jew?"

"He died."

The council stared at Jeanine with open hostility. She felt lightheaded and dizzy, as though she might faint. It seemed that her case was most hopeless. Just then the doors opened behind her, and to everyone's surprise Victor Pindar entered the room with Simon Grosz at his side.

"I would like to address this council," Victor announced. Jeanine's breath caught in her throat. He hadn't deserted her.

"And who might you be?"

"I am Victor Pindar, and this gentleman is Simon Grosz." Victor paused and grinned. "The dead man of whom you speak."

The gasps of surprise were welcome sounds in Jeanine's ears, but no more so than the sight of Simon. She wanted to run to him—to both of them. Simon was alive! She eyed him suspiciously for any signs of his failing health, but he only smiled at her as if to reassure her of his strength.

"You are the Jew?" the bishop asked curiously.

"I am he," Simon admitted, coming to stand in front of the council.

"Monsieur Colbert, you told this council that the Jew had fallen victim to the practices of witchcraft."

"Can you not see? The witch brought him back to life. She has powers that far exceed our imaginings," Colbert declared, then crossed himself for emphasis.

"What say you of this, mademoiselle?" the bishop asked Jeanine.

"I am innocent," Jeanine answered as evenly as she could. Her heart was pounding with anticipation of her freedom. Surely now that Simon was here, the council could see Colbert's lies for themselves.

"Mademoiselle de la Fontaine," the bishop began, "will you tell this council what purpose you had for consorting with this Jew?"

Jeanine swallowed hard. The easy thing would be to lie, but she'd pledged to God and to herself that no more lies would pass through her lips. She glanced at Simon, whose very existence could be threatened by her telling of the truth. He nodded knowingly, as if to assure her that honesty could harm neither of them. Turning back to the council, she faced Colbert's sneering expression. There was pure hatred in his eyes as she answered, "I went there for the purpose of learning."

"Learning? Pray tell, what would you have a Jew teach you?"

"Simon is a physician," Jeanine said flatly. "I went to him in order to help him with his work for the poor. Many of the dockworkers and their families had fallen ill with no hope of affording proper care. Simon offered them his assistance in whatever manner he could, and I in turn offered my help."

"What help did you suppose yourself capable of?"

Jeanine finally allowed her gaze to travel to where Victor stood silently watching. He was dressed in a dark green cotehardie which reached just below his hips to meet black hose and boots. His dark hair was still wind-blown from his ride to the estate, but his eyes were eager to encourage her. He looked to be completely healed of his wounds, and in the healthy glow of his face, she found an expression of compassion that she had never known.

Her strength was renewed. God had not allowed her to face the council without support. Not only was He in His heaven watching over her, but He had sent her family and her one true love to stand beside her throughout her ordeal.

"I felt myself called to learn of Simon's medical knowledge."

The bored-looking physicians seemed to take new notice in this declaration. The leader, an aged man with thick mounds of wavy gray hair, held up his hand to enter the conversation. "You say you desired to learn of the Jew's medical knowledge? What possible wisdom could he have in this field?"

"He is a physician. He trained at the university in Montpellier."

"That may well have been the case, but Jews are not allowed to practice medicine under the laws of our country. Laws, which I might add, are most clearly given for a purpose."

"This man is most gifted, and he helps those who cannot afford the care of *legal* physicians such as yourself." Jeanine felt her anger mounting. It was enough that they should attack her, but to impugn Simon as well was more than she was willing to stand. "This man has saved hundreds of lives and should be held in your esteem instead of your contempt."

"I see. And do you consider yourself a physician as well?" the doctor asked her in a cynical voice.

Jeanine paused, looked over her shoulder at her family, and took in a deep breath. "I do."

The council again began murmuring together, and this time, the physicians joined in. The bishop held up his hand for silence. "By what authority do you make these claims? Have you proof of your work with the Jew?"

"I claim no authority except that which is given by the Lord God in heaven. As for my work, how could I yet prove it while standing here before you? I could recite the dealings of the body. Speak to you of humors and the anatomy which designs each human being. I can tell you of binding wounds and setting bones, of surgical procedures to save the lives of the dying, but what proof can I offer you?"

"I stand as her proof," Victor offered, coming forward with long even strides. "I submit myself before the physicians of this board. I was injured in a storm at sea. I sustained some form of head injury—I'm certain Mademoiselle de la Fontaine could be more precise about the details."

He pulled back the thick dark hair that had fallen in an

unruly manner across his forehead. "Here at the temple I received a desperate blow, and here is the place where the pressure was relieved when the blood pressed in against my brain."

The leading physician stood up and came to examine Victor's head. "Trephining is a most delicate surgery which requires a great deal of skill and training. Would you have me believe that this woman acted out such a procedure? I'd sooner believe the Jew capable of this."

"Ask her yourself, but I know she saved my life." Victor's gaze found hers and lingered for several moments on her face. He smiled, and there was such tenderness in his expression that Jeanine felt herself flushing. He knew what she'd done, and he didn't appear in the least disturbed by it. What manner of man was he? Could he truly accept this passion of hers?

"Is it true?" the bishop finally asked when the physician seemed to become more fascinated by Victor's new scars than in interrogating the defendant.

Jeanine nodded. "*Oui.* I performed the surgery with the assistance and direction of Dr. Grosz." She heard her mother gasp and longed to turn and offer further explanation, but Antoine chose that moment to seal her doom.

"Your Grace, can this be anything other than the proof you need? She admits to holding life and death in her hands. She admits to performing acts of surgery upon the flesh of this man. What more do you need to show evidence that my accusations are true?"

The bishop nodded. "You make a valid point, sir, but I have yet another question to ask of this woman." He paused. "By whose authority have you gained your power?"

Jeanine's chin tilted upward in confidence. "By the Lord God Almighty."

"Blasphemy!" Colbert declared. "She speaks blasphemy.

The devil is her god."

"You are wrong, monsieur," Jeanine said, shaking her head. "I serve only the Lord God in Heaven."

"She lies, I tell you," Colbert said, taking a stand between Jeanine and the bishop. "The church gives no recognition of women as physicians. Our own laws declare it illegal for women to practice medicine, and Holy Scriptures demand our obedience unto the laws of the land. How, therefore, can this woman speak the truth and accredit her acts to God? She is the devil's handmaiden, I tell you."

At this, Jeanine's father protested loudly, as did her brother. Victor had stepped away from the board of physicians and made several menacing steps towards Colbert.

"Enough!" the bishop demanded. "The council will speak on this matter in private. I believe we have heard sufficient words on this day." He turned to the board of physicians and continued. "We will retire and hear your thoughts on this matter. I shall give my decision within the hour." At that, he and the other members of the clergy rose to their feet and exited the great room.

Jeanine let out a long breath, not even aware that she'd been holding it the entire time of the bishop's departure. She watched as the physicians followed the clergy. All seemed to eye her with contempt, and not even one offered her so much as a single word of acknowledgment. Colbert waited until they had gone to motion his men to take Jeanine in hand. Victor quickly came to her side and met Colbert head-on.

"She stays here," Victor said, taking hold of Jeanine's arm. "You have seen her imprisoned for the past month, and that is more than enough."

"She is a witch," Colbert said, glaring in defiance.

"I stand to defend this woman's honor," Victor replied, drawing Jeanine ever closer. "I should call you out for your words and run a sword through your heart."

Colbert laughed. " 'Twould be your own death, monsieur." He eyed Victor for a moment as if trying to decide whether the battle would be worth the effort, then waved his arms in acceptance. "Have it your way. Let her say her good-byes and farewells. 'Tis of little consequence to me."

Victor turned to Jeanine and led her to where her family stood anxiously waiting. Jeanine longed to remain at Victor's side, but at the sight of her mother's open arms, she fled one haven for another. "Oh, ma *mère*," she sobbed against her mother's frail shoulder, "I am so sorry for the lies I told you."

"Hush now. All is forgiven," her mother whispered.

Jeanine felt her father's sturdy hand upon her head. "Has he harmed you, daughter?"

She raised her tear-filled eyes and shook her head. "*Non.* He feared the excommunication promised by the priest should he lay a hand upon me. Of course, that warning did nothing to close his mouth from the rude and wicked things he said to me."

Victor and Étienne had come to stand directly behind her, and Jeanine turned to meet their dear faces. "I am so sorry to have brought this upon our house. It was only my desire to help people. Truly, I sought only to serve God through the work of my hands." She wiped at her tears with her sleeve. "I was foolish not to realize that by lying I was also serving Satan's purpose. No matter what happens this day, I will not forget what you have done." She said this as if collectively for the group, which now included Simon as well. But it was to Victor that she directed her gaze.

Already she could hear the commotion of the physicians and clergy as they made their way back into the great hall. They had been gone only minutes, instead of the promised hour. She began to tremble, seeing the stern, unyielding expressions on each of their faces. Her doom was certain, and in that moment, she realized that they would demand her death. Colbert's men pushed Victor and her family aside and took Jeanine roughly in hand to bring her before the table where the men were now assembling.

"Jeanine de la Fontaine," the bishop addressed her with an arrogance that left her cold, "by your own admission you have willfully performed the acts of surgery and the concocting of potions. Because there is no evidence in Scripture that God would allow a woman the power of life and death in the actions of a physician, it may only be assumed that your power is from Satan himself."

"No!" Jeanine cried out and the men at her sides tightened their hold.

"Silence!" the bishop demanded. "You have admitted to consorting with a Jew, a man whom we all know to have no faith in the risen Christ. You have admitted to taking on his teachings, and therefore you have made yourself a heretic in the sight of the church. You have willingly participated in the manipulation of human flesh and held power over those in your care, and therefore have provided evidence to this council that you are given over to the powers of your dark lord, Satan."

"No! 'Tis a lie! I denounce Satan. I serve God alone," Jeanine declared, struggling against the hold Colbert's henchmen kept on her.

The bishop ignored her. "It is the decision of this council that you be burned at the stake upon the dawning of the morning sun, for the practice of witchcraft. May God have mercy on your soul."

Jeanine felt her chest tighten and the room began to swirl around her. They were going through with this. They were really going to put her to death, and all because she had tried to heal the sick. She felt her vision dim and a sensation of heat overwhelmed her. In her mind's eye she felt the flames lick at her face as she lost consciousness and fell limp between her captors.

fourteen

Victor longed to dislodge the unconscious Jeanine from the grip of Colbert's henchmen, but he knew he had little hope of doing so. He stepped forward just as Jeanine's mother and father rushed to the bishop to plead for their daughter's life.

"Your Grace, she's not a witch," Madame de la Fontaine declared, sobbing out her words with the broken heart of a mother. "She is but a girl, and her heart is pure."

"She is just a child," François de la Fontaine added. "Our only daughter."

"Unless it is your desire to burn at her side, you will leave this council and accept her fate. She has admitted to her guilt, even if her intentions were otherwise. The church cannot accept such behavior in its people, and your daughter cannot be allowed to live only to corrupt the souls of others."

Colbert watched with seeming indifference. He turned to find Victor openly watching him, then motioned to his men to leave Jeanine upon the floor. They did so, unceremoniously dropping her to the cold hard stones before throwing Victor a glance that dared his interference.

Victor clenched his teeth tightly and prayed for heavenly intervention. He wanted very badly to pull the sword at his side and run each of the men through before separating Colbert's head from his body. But instead of acting upon those feelings, Victor held his ground. For Jeanine's sake, he would find a way to rescue her. Mindless of Colbert's watchful eye and self-satisfied expression, Victor moved past the guards and went to where Jeanine lay.

Tenderly, he turned her and lifted her still form in his arms. He carried her to the place where her family had sat to watch her mock trial, and there he cradled her until her mother came to him.

"I think you have come to care a great deal for my daughter, *non?*" the older woman questioned. Her eyes were red from crying, but her face was ashen white. Fear etched itself deeply in her countenance.

"I do," Victor admitted. He looked down upon Jeanine's delicate features and wondered why it was that she had ever fallen in love with him. There had been nothing between them save her desire to keep him from death. By her own admission many others had been saved by her hand, so what made him different? Why had she gazed upon his face and lost her heart?

Madame de la Fontaine stroked her daughter's face and called to her. "Jeanine. Jeanine. Wake up, my little angel."

Jeanine stirred in Victor's arms, and her eyelids fluttered open. She smiled up at Victor as if finding herself in his arms was a commonplace thing. She closed her eyes again, and Victor was glad for the moment to compose himself. Her trusting smile had pierced his heart. She could count on him to save her life, even as she had saved his.

"Jeanine, wake up," her mother said again, and this time she gently patted her daughter's cheeks.

"What?" Jeanine questioned drowsily, opening her eyes again. She looked around at the people now gathered, and realization began to dawn upon her. Her face took on an expression of sheer terror, and Victor found himself helpless to soothe her fears.

"They are going to kill me," she declared and pushed away from Victor. He eased her onto the bench beside him, but kept a hand on her arm as if to calm her.

"You must have faith," her mother told her, tears flowing anew. "We must have faith."

Étienne came to put an arm around his mother, even as his father joined them and announced, "Colbert has put us from his lands. We may witness the execution on the morrow, but we will not be allowed to remain with her through the night. Jeanine is to be taken back to her tower room and there. . ." He could say no more.

Margarite de la Fontaine began to sob in earnest, and Étienne gently handed her over to his father. "We must take Mama from this place," he advised his father. "Trust Victor and me to work through the details."

"Might I offer my assistance?" Simon questioned in a whisper.

Étienne nodded. "We will need all the help we can get."

Colbert came up at that moment. "Take this Jew from my house, and all of you go. I want no interference in this matter. Monsieur de la Fontaine, I will expect payment in full on the morrow for your debts." He acted as if to leave them, then turned around and motioned to his henchmen. "Escort them from the estate."

François cast a quick glance upon his daughter. "I love you, my child. God will be with us."

Jeanine nodded. "I love you, *mon père*."

"Do not lose faith," her mother managed to say between mournful wails.

"I won't, *ma mère*. I love you." Jeanine suddenly became the strong one.

Étienne leaned down and kissed her upon the forehead. "I will return."

"I love you, Étienne," she said, and Victor noted the desperation in her voice. It wasn't fear; it was urgency to say that which might never be said again.

Simon was already being led from the room when the

second guard took hold of François de la Fontaine and gave him a powerful push toward the door. "Leave the witch now," he ordered.

Jeanine's father tried one final time to appeal to Colbert, and Victor took that moment to turn to Jeanine. He took in the huge worried eyes, so dark and velvety in their brown depths that for a moment he could forget her plight. He reached up a hand and touched her cheek, and instantly he claimed Jeanine's attention.

"Five geese flying," he whispered, his lips barely inches from hers. He saw her eyes widen in surprise, just before he kissed her soundly upon the mouth. "I will come for you," he said, pulling away.

Jeanine's hand flew up to touch her lips. She was obviously overwhelmed with her feelings for what had just taken place. Colbert's angry denial of Monsieur de la Fontaine's pleadings caused Victor to realize he hadn't much time. "I love you."

"Oh, Victor, I love you, too. You are my heart."

"Do not be afraid," he told her confidently. "I will find a way to set you free."

❧

From the moment Victor had declared his love for her, Jeanine found a peace of mind that made facing her own execution not quite so fearful. She had marveled at his confirmation of feelings that she had long only dreamed might be given her. Now, as she hugged her arms to her body and watched for the first light of dawn, Jeanine knew that God was with her and that she had nothing to fear.

"Death cannot take love from me," she whispered and leaned back against the cold stones of the wall. "Not God's love, nor Victor's, nor that of my family. I have known much love in my short life, and should all else fail and my death be required, I will face my fate with the assurance that God has been ever faithful."

Since the time Colbert had seen her thrown back into this room, Jeanine had contemplated Victor's words and her own future. "I trust you, Father God," she prayed. "I believe in Your power to bring me out of this nightmare, but if it is not Your will, I accept that as well." She glanced back out the tiny slit of a window. The black skies remained as confirmation that her presence on earth might yet continue a while longer.

"I don't want to die," she whispered, but this time her eyes remained dry as she lifted her gaze upward. "I give You my heart and soul and mind, Father. I give You all that I am or ever hope to be. I commend my spirit into Your keeping, even as I did as a small child. I beg Your mercy for my family, and ask that You might comfort them in this hour, even as You have comforted me."

She smoothed down the thin linen cloth of the unbelted white houppeland which she'd been given to face her execution in. Her head covering had been taken from her, and her curly brown hair had been left to flow freely around her. Colbert intended to humiliate her in her final hour, but in truth, Jeanine found no embarrassment in her condition. She had remained faithful. She had refused to lie, even though it meant her life.

She glanced out the window again, and her heart lurched. The tiniest thread of color imposed itself upon the far horizon. Her time had come.

As if on cue, she heard the bar lift, and the guard pushed back the door. "You are to come," he said solemnly.

Jeanine nodded and followed the man down the spiral stairs. She wondered if her family would be allowed to come to her, and whether she could offer any comfort to them. Walking slowly behind the sober-faced guard, Jeanine kept remembering Victor's last words. He had used her code with Simon. *Five geese flying.* She forced herself to think of her grandmother's stories and of the significance of such symbolism. Concentrating on these things, Jeanine found the strength to go forward.

She was led into the courtyard and just beyond the stables, and it was here that she found Colbert and the priest awaiting her. The skies were barely touched with blue, and the sun had not yet appeared above the horizon.

"I have come to hear your confession, my child," the priest said sympathetically.

"Thank you, Father, but I have already made my peace with God," Jeanine said defiantly.

"Demons cannot make peace with God," Colbert said, sneering at her.

Jeanine smiled ever so slightly. "You should know, monsieur."

She walked past them and caught sight of the post that had been erected for her execution. A small platform had been nailed approximately five feet off the ground. This would allow for the bundles of wood and straw to be placed beneath her feet, while Jeanine stood on the platform, hands bound to the post at her back.

She swallowed hard, fear threatening to take away her composure. *God is with me,* she reminded herself. *Nothing Colbert or his men can do can take that from me.*

fifteen

The priest came to stand beside Jeanine, and without asking her permission, he made the sign of the cross and offered up prayers on behalf of her soul. "Do you renounce Satan?" he asked.

Jeanine looked fiercely at Colbert and answered, "I do now, as I always have."

"Do you accept the one true God?" the priest continued.

"I do."

"Do you now seek absolution from your sins?"

Jeanine heard Colbert snort as if to hold back laughter. "I have already been absolved," Jeanine replied. "I have given my spirit over to God, and it is well with my soul."

The priest seemed momentarily stunned by her response. He made the sign of the cross again and lifted a crucifix to Jeanine's face. *"Sis mortuus mundo, vivens iterum Deo."*

Be thou dead to this world, living again to God. Jeanine smiled, recognizing the Latin words and remembering Simon's diligence to teach her the language as an aide to her medical training. The bittersweet memory flooded her soul, along with a deep regret that she might never live to know Victor's love in full. She scanned the horizon for any sign of her love or her family, but there was none to be found.

"Let us finish this before there is trouble," Colbert demanded. "Who knows what treachery her family has planned?"

The church council assembled at the table Colbert had prepared for them. There was a good distance between them and the execution platform, but Jeanine knew they would have little trouble confirming that their orders were being carried out in full.

Colbert grabbed her arm roughly, and Jeanine shuddered at his touch. He laughed. "You could have found yourself considerably better cared for, had you not denied me."

"I would have naught but misery in your presence," she replied.

He stopped, eyed her contemptuously for a moment, then shrugged. "You have made your own fate. You chose to live by your hand, and now you will die by mine. It seems just fair that I should have the final say in this matter."

"You have no say in this matter at all, monsieur," Jeanine countered. "God in heaven holds the keys to life and death. You, Antoine Colbert, are but a pawn in His game. You think to outwit God, to force your will upon Him and His people, but you are gravely mistaken." She faced him bravely, not caring how he might respond to her. "I have known the love of family and friends and of a godly man. You cannot take that from me, even if you take my life."

"You are a foolish woman," Colbert declared. "You might have saved your life had you but yielded to me. I feel nothing but contempt for you now." He spat in her face and turned to walk away.

"And I feel nothing but pity for you, monsieur," Jeanine called after him. She saw his shoulders stiffen and knew her words had hit their mark. Her sense of peace offended him. No doubt he had hoped to have her beg for mercy and fall upon him for salvation.

The guard was again at her side. He motioned her forward, and when they stood beside the execution post, he gently lifted her thinly clad body and positioned her bare feet on the platform. On a ladder that had been placed behind her, Jeanine could glance around to find still another guard preparing to bind her hands with leather thongs. Below her, a bevy of servants worked at a feverish pitch to mound dry wood and bundles of straw.

Colbert had taken his place with the bishop, and Jeanine refused to give in to the look of triumph upon his face. God would save her. Whether it be in the midst of flames as He took her spirit up to heaven, or in the miraculous rescue that Victor had promised.

The priest again appeared below her to offer up prayers on her behalf. Jeanine felt desperation edging out her confidence. *I can do this,* she promised herself. *I can stand strong in the face of this false accusation because God knows my innocence.* She took a deep breath and caught the priest's sympathetic expression.

"What of my parents?" Jeanine dared to ask.

The priest shrugged. "It is better this way, *non?* 'Twould be difficult for them to observe their child burned alive."

Jeanine swallowed hard. Victor and Étienne had promised to return, but there was no sign of them or anyone else who might offer her love in her final moments. Sweat formed on her brow, and her stomach churned with revolting anxiety.

"Let us finish this thing," Colbert called out. "The sun is now in the sky." Colbert's guards formed two straight lines behind him.

The bishop nodded and offered the final words. "Jeanine de la Fontaine, for the sin of consorting with the devil, you are hereby sentenced to death by the purging of your soul and flesh in fire. As the Scripture of our Lord tells us in Revelation, 'Blessed are they that do his commandments, that they may have right to the tree of life, and may enter in through the gates into the city. For without are dogs, and sorcerers, and whoremongers, and murderers, and idolaters, and whosoever loveth and maketh a lie.' "

Jeanine felt the words pierce her soul. She had been one to make lies a daily part of her life, and now she was paying the penalty. But even as she thought this, God filled her heart with peace, and she recalled the words of Psalm 6: *Siegneur, ne me reprenez pas dans votre fureur, et ne me chatiez pas dans votre colere*—O Lord, rebuke me not in thine anger, neither chasten me in thy hot displeasure. *Ayez pitié de moi, Seigneur, parce que je suis faible*—Have mercy upon me, O Lord; for I am weak. The words seemed to flow through her mind with ease, and Jeanine began to murmur them loud enough for the man who bound her hands to hear her.

"Heal me; for my bones are vexed. My soul is also sore vexed: but thou, O Lord, how long? Return, O Lord, deliver my soul: oh save me for thy mercies' sake. For in death there is no remembrance of thee; in the grave who shall give thee thanks?"

The man tied her hands loosely. His touch was infinitely tender. He leaned forward and whispered, "God have mercy on you, mademoiselle."

"Merci," she replied, touched by his kindness.

Turning her gaze back upon the bishop and Colbert, Jeanine faced her impending execution. She watched as a burning torch was brought forth by one of Colbert's men. He halted before the bishop, who appeared to bless the man and the fire.

Then, even as she watched the scene unfold before her, Jeanine heard something in the distance. Turning her head to the south, she saw the unmistakable rise of dust marking the approach of riders. The noise increased, and the thundering sound left little doubt that the number of riders was great.

"Burn the witch!" Colbert cried out and motioned to his

guards to take up their positions. But it was too late. Much to Colbert's surprise, Victor Pindar and Étienne de la Fontaine appeared on horseback from behind the stables. The army approaching from the south seemed to be their signal to reveal their presence.

"Burn her!" Colbert raged and moved forward to take the torch in hand for himself.

The man behind Jeanine quickly cut her bonds and pointed to Victor's approaching mount. Victor rode up beside the execution platform and motioned to Jeanine. "Jump!" he declared, as the bondman saluted him.

"I do not understand," Jeanine said, turning to the man who was now climbing down the ladder to take up arms on behalf of Victor.

"Jump to me," Victor demanded and held out his arms.

Jeanine hesitated a moment, but as Colbert touched the torch to brittle wood, she knew there was no other choice. She threw herself out, pushing off the platform with as much force as she could muster.

"Stop them!" Colbert screamed. His guards advanced on Victor's horse, just as Jeanine flung herself into Victor's awaiting arms.

There was no time for Victor to settle her properly on his mount. He spurred the horse into action and moved away even as the clang of swords rang out against their scabbards.

"Hold tight," he yelled in her ear, to be heard above the din. The army who had come to their rescue was moving into position to offer them protection and coverage.

"Who are those men?" she asked, clinging desperately to Victor's neck, her legs flailing wildly behind her and slapping at the horse's side.

He laughed. "Tell you later." With one fluid motion, he slipped his hand beneath her legs and hoisted her into position in front of him. "Better?"

"Much," she admitted.

Jeanine buried her face against Victor's neck as they raced ahead to meet the front line of their defense. Étienne was quickly beside them with a roar of raging men following up behind.

"Better pick up the pace," he called to Victor, "or you'll never live long enough to become my brother-in-law."

Victor chuckled, and his amusement lessened Jeanine's fear. They both seemed so confident of their ability to take charge of the day that it gave her cause for hope.

"I'll stay here with the others," Étienne added, "and I'll meet you both at the agreed-upon place."

"God be with you," Victor answered, and Jeanine glanced up to watch Étienne fall behind them to join the ranks of the small army.

For several minutes they rode in silence. Jeanine knew from the direction they'd taken that they were headed south, farther away from Bruges. Still stunned by the suddenness of her rescue, she was further surprised when Victor slowed his mount.

"What is this?" she questioned. "You have slowed. Colbert will catch us."

"I think not," Victor replied. "The king's men will busy him."

"The king's men?" Jeanine questioned.

"Aye."

"I don't understand," she said, shifting her weight. She was painfully aware of her light linen gown billowing out around her. Modestly, she tucked the edges of the skirt beneath her as best she could.

"You hardly need to," Victor told her. He slowed the horse even more and stared down into her face. "It is enough that you are safely here in my arms."

She felt her face grow hot, even as she became aware that he was going to kiss her. His kiss was tender and searching, as if seeking answers for questions that he'd not yet voiced. She wrapped her arms around him and pressed closer. *Would that such feelings could go on forever,* she thought.

"Thank you for saving my life," she murmured, as he pulled away. It was the only safe thing she could think of to say.

"I was indebted to you," he said, eyeing her curiously. "I remember you as Dr. Font, but I cannot imagine how I mistook you for a man."

She laughed, and it sounded good in her own ears to be filled with such joy. "You were most gravely injured and heavily drugged with our concoctions. It is not hard to imagine that you saw me as a man. It is a wonder you saw or remembered anything at all."

"I remember you blessing me. It was the one thing that stuck out in my mind. Then that night when you were fleeing your marriage to Colbert, you offered up the same blessing upon me again."

"I remember," she said, feeling suddenly shy. "I wanted very much for you to know me. To know how much I cared."

Victor halted the horse and looked at her with great perplexity. "How is it that you came to care for me?"

She smiled. "I was drawn to you from the moment of our first meeting. I appeared upon the *Crispin,* in disguise of course, and my brother led me to your litter. I found you there, dying from your wounds, and never have I felt the things for another that I felt for you that day."

"But why? Certainly the face of a dying man could mean nothing to you but yet another patient."

She shrugged. "I know not why my heart chose you. I

only know that the feeling never left me."

"What feeling is that?" asked Victor, still appearing to scrutinize her words for solutions to the puzzle.

Jeanine threw caution to the wind. If he found offense in her words, then at least she would have been honest with him. If he rejected her then, it would be painful, but certainly less so than were there to be lies between them. "The feeling that we were destined to be together. That I would always love you. That I would find my greatest happiness with you."

"I see." Victor grew strangely silent. He urged the horse forward, still lost in thought.

"When did you come to care for me?" Jeanine finally asked, desperate for the silence to be filled.

Victor laughed, and tiny lines formed around his eyes. Jeanine thought they made him look even more handsome than he already was. "I'm not sure I can say exactly. It might have been when you came into my room that night. You were so brave and noble about the entire matter, giving me over your prized possessions, all in order to save your father from certain destruction."

Noises from behind them alerted Victor that he'd been too lax in his duties. "Hold fast. We're being pursued."

Jeanine's heart picked up speed. She dared to glance over her shoulder and found several mounted men, including Antoine Colbert, bearing down upon them. *Dear Father in heaven,* she prayed, *help us to escape our enemies.* Psalm 6 came to mind once again, and she remembered the final verses of the passage with hope: *The Lord hath heard my supplication; the Lord will receive my prayer. Let all mine enemies be ashamed and sore vexed: let them return and be ashamed suddenly.*

Jeanine didn't care that Colbert be punished for his actions against her. She longed only that she be allowed to escape without harm to herself, Victor, or her brother. Then, too, she thought, there were the men of the king's army. She whispered a prayer for their safety and asked God's blessings on all who had befriended her cause, but even as the words were thought, she noticed that Victor's horse was tiring under the strain of two riders. Colbert was gaining ground.

sixteen

It was evident to Victor that outdistancing Colbert would be impossible. He chided himself for his lax attitude and assumption that he could simply ride in and take Jeanine without any trouble coming upon them.

"I'll have to fight him," Victor told Jeanine and reined back on the horse so hard that the animal cried out in fear and reared wildly. Jeanine tightened her grip on Victor, but already he was maneuvering to put her from the horse. "Go into the trees. Stay out of sight. If you remain out here, someone might take you from me."

Jeanine slid down the side of the horse, her face a ghastly shade of white. "Oh, Victor, no! I cannot lose you now."

"Have faith, Jeanine. I once was quite handy with a sword. I have no reason to believe myself incompetent now."

Colbert and his men had slowed a safe distance from Victor and Jeanine. Victor cast a quick glance from them to Jeanine and back again. In the distance he could see pursuing riders. Either Étienne had come to his defense, or they were friends of Colbert. Either way, Victor didn't want to wait and see. He reached behind him and pulled his sword free. He thrilled to the sound of the metal as it passed from the scabbard and into the air. The ring persuaded him that he was capable of meeting any match.

Ahead, he could see Colbert's expression change from satisfaction and victorious pursuit to one of fear and assessment. Colbert halted his horse's progress and appeared to contemplate the matter. The men at his side matched the action of their leader and brought their own animals to a stop. The rotund man scratched his belly, then drew his sword and laughed at what surely appeared a hopeless attempt on Victor's part to protect Jeanine.

"Dear God," Victor prayed, "if ever Your help was needed, 'tis now. Remember me Your servant this day. Give unto me the victory that I might glorify Your name. Amen." Confidence surged through Victor. He glanced over his shoulder and saw that Jeanine had made her way to the trees. The time had come.

Victor balanced the sword carefully in his hands, then swung it around in a circle over his head and gave a fierce battle cry. Sinking his heels into the horse's flanks, he held fast as the animal leaped into action.

Colbert and his men were so intent on Victor's display, that they failed to notice Étienne and six other mounted men approach from behind. The men were nearly upon them just as Victor came within proper fighting distance of Colbert. Wielding his weapon, Victor brought the sword down hard, as if to cleave Colbert in half. The sound of metal upon metal rang out in the early morning country-side as Colbert's sword intervened and kept the older man from death.

Étienne and his men busied Colbert's guard while Victor faced off with Colbert. The horses whinnied and pranced nervously as the men lunged and pressed their war upon each other. At one point, Colbert lurched sideways to deflect Victor's blow. Hopelessly off balance, Colbert tumbled from the side of his horse and narrowly escaped being stepped on by the beast as it fled the battlefield.

Victor swung his own mount around and jumped from its back. The match was now to be on foot, and Victor could see that Colbert could barely lift his weapon. His weight and age were clearly against him. Victor thought to offer him mercy. It was evident that the rest of Colbert's guard were being soundly defeated.

Sweat poured from his face as he called out, "Do you yield? Will you leave us to go in peace?"

Colbert laughed haughtily. "Never! I will kill the witch myself after I run you through." He lunged, but Victor easily dodged the sword.

"It is not my desire to take your life, monsieur," Victor replied, "but I will not allow you to kill my intended bride."

"Bride, ha!" Colbert gasped for air before continuing. "She will never be yours."

He raised up his sword and brought it down hard, but Victor jumped to the side while slicing his own weapon through the air. The sword caught Colbert's left arm, and a thin strip of material fell away. Blood immediately oozed from the wound, but this only served to infuriate Colbert.

"She has been condemned in the eyes of the church. Condemned to death," Colbert said, his thick chest heaving up and down with every swing of his blade. "Who will marry you, should you live? They will only seek you out, and then both of you will die."

"She is no witch, as well you know. You have lied in the sight of God and His witnesses," Victor said, thrusting the blade forward. He pierced the sword arm of Colbert and felt the edge of his sword hit bone.

Colbert screamed in anguish. His arm appeared useless as his sword fell to the dirt. Victor took that moment to halt the fight. He stood panting lightly, watching Colbert intently.

"Will you yield now, man? You are wounded, and I have no desire to cause you further harm."

Colbert refused to acknowledge him. His loud wailing and groans made it evident that he was completely spent. Victor glanced up to find Étienne looking down on him from atop his horse.

"Sorry we let him slip through. The home guard was a bit of a challenge," Étienne offered by way of explanation.

" 'Tis my fault as well for slowing the horse. I should have kept my thoughts on what we were about, instead of romancing your little sister," Victor admitted.

Colbert's wound was bleeding profusely, and Victor motioned to Étienne. "Tear a strip from one of his men's tunics. We should bind the arm."

Étienne nodded and turned his horse to ride back to where Colbert's men were now disarmed and bound. Victor thought only to assure himself of Jeanine's safety, and without concern for Colbert, he too turned his back upon the older man.

He walked less than two paces when the hairs on the back of his neck prickled and Jeanine's scream rent the air. Turning, sword poised, Victor met Colbert as he charged. Colbert flailed the sword aimless in his left hand, while Victor's weapon remained sure and steady. There was no stopping the man's onslaught, and Victor winced as his sword buried itself deep in the man's chest. Colbert dropped his own blade and reached dumbly for the sword now sticking out of his body. He opened his mouth, then fell over backward.

Victor pulled his sword out and knelt beside the man. "It need not have ended this way, Colbert. You had but to let us depart in peace."

"Curse you and the witch," Colbert said. "Be gone from me and let my own attend my wounds."

"You need a physician." Victor stood and caught sight of Jeanine waiting faithfully by the trees. He wiped the bloody sword against his boot and made his way to where she stood, still covering her mouth with her hands.

"Colbert is wounded—mortally, I fear," Victor told her gravely.

Jeanine fell into his arms, a sob breaking from her throat. "I thought he would kill you. I thought—"

"Shhh," he whispered against her ear. " 'Tis well with me, but that man will bleed to death if he doesn't have a doctor's care soon."

Jeanine straightened. "I will go to him."

Victor stared at her in silence. "Dare you say that *you* propose to see to his wounds?"

"I am a physician, whether legal or elsewise. If his wounds are that grave, there is scarce time to return him to his estate, much less bring a doctor from Bruges."

Victor smiled, his heart warmed by her ability to tend her enemy. "Come then." He put an arm around her and drew her along.

Victor had nearly reached Colbert's side when the wounded man screamed out in pain, "Get the witch away from me!"

Jeanine ignored him and squatted down beside his quivering form. "Monsieur, you are wounded. Let me attend to you."

"I would rather die," he said hatefully. Gasping for air, he tried to roll away from her touch.

"You *will* die if I am not allowed to help you. This wound is severe."

" 'Tis your doing, witch. My death will be upon your head." Colbert shifted, groaning miserably as his life's blood drained from his body. "My men will testify to your treachery."

"What can they do to me?" Jeanine asked softly and got to her feet. She stared down at Colbert as if anticipating an answer. "You have condemned me to death already, yet God has interceded on my behalf. With God so obviously for me, what can you or any mere man do to cause me harm?"

Colbert spat at her and again insisted that one of his

own men be allowed to tend his wounds. Victor finally agreed and called to Étienne. "Release the man who is least injured and bring him to tend his master."

While Étienne took up this task, Victor reached for Jeanine. "Come. We must make for safety. Colbert is right in saying that others will soon be summoned to find us."

Jeanine nodded and fixed her gaze on him in such a way that Victor wanted very much to crush her to him and kiss her long and lovingly. He found her trust so rewarding, so faithful. She reminded him in many ways of his sister. Loyal, true, trusting.

"Where will we go?" she asked, and Victor knew instantly it wasn't offered as a question of doubt.

"We have it all worked out," he assured her. "You have only to trust me."

She smiled warmly and looped her arm through his. " 'Tis no difficult task to do that. I would follow you to the ends of the earth."

"And well you may," he teased, pulling her back to where his horse mindlessly nibbled on the grass. He lifted Jeanine up on the horse, then climbed on behind her. "Étienne, let us be off," he called. "These good men will see to Colbert's wounds and give us the time we need to get ourselves to safety."

Jeanine eyed the six riderless horses. " 'Twould make more sense, my love, if we were to take up one of the other horses to aid our cause," she said.

"They would only add thievery to our list of wrongs," Victor told her seriously. Then turning her in the saddle so that she fit more neatly against him, he smiled. "Besides, I like this so much more."

Jeanine pressed her face against his neck and sighed. "*Oui,* it is most acceptable."

seventeen

Jeanine felt her sense of security slip from her as they neared Bruges. Victor had tried to reassure her that all was well under control, but she still feared for her life and his. Ever in the back of her mind was the worry that they could never find peace again in their lives. She had been condemned as a witch. No matter where she went, that past would haunt her and rise against their happiness.

Victor maneuvered the horse into a narrow alleyway and waited while Étienne slid from his mount and reached up for Jeanine. Jeanine grew fearful for a moment, thinking that Victor intended to leave them while he went elsewhere. To her relief, however, he dismounted and tossed the reins to a gangly boy who had materialized out of a darkened shop doorway.

"Do you know what to do with these beasts?" he asked the boy.

Jeanine saw the boy nod. "You can count on me, monsieur. Simon told me where to hide them."

"Good enough," Victor replied. He motioned to Étienne and pushed Jeanine toward the open door. "We'll go here first and change our clothes. I wouldn't want you to catch your death from the light weight of that gown."

Jeanine felt her face grow hot. So he had noticed the thinness of the houppeland. Embarrassed, she longed for nothing more than a heavy cloak or cotehardie. To her surprise, she was offered both once they were inside the shop. A woman not so much older than Jeanine came to them. " 'Tis well-worn, but I have a gown for the lady.

Come with me."

Jeanine glanced up at Victor and then to her brother. "Go on," Victor encouraged. "And be quick about it. We haven't much time."

Jeanine hurried into the back room with the woman, and rather than strip off the white linen gown, she pulled a very plain, sideless surcoat over her head. The dark brown material fell against her execution gown in stark contrast, but Jeanine didn't care. The woman handed her a simple woolen cap before offering to braid her hair.

"You are very kind to help me," Jeanine murmured. "Thank you."

"You saved the life of my father," the young woman said, pulling the thick bulk of Jeanine's hair into some semblance of order.

"Me?"

"*Oui.* He was on the *Crispin.* His leg was badly crushed. You had to remove it, but at least he didn't bleed to death or take on poisoning of the blood. 'Tis a small way to offer you thanks."

"I remember him well," Jeanine responded thoughtfully. " 'Twould be my great pleasure to see him again."

"You will when the time is right. He has agreed to help see you to safety." She finished Jeanine's hair and waited while Jeanine secured her cap in place. "I have a cloak for you by the back door. It should allow you to slip through town unnoticed."

"Again, you have my thanks," Jeanine said, taking hold of the woman's shoulder. "I feel quite blessed to call you friend."

The woman blushed and waved Jeanine off. "You'd best be gone now. No doubt they'll be searching for you."

Jeanine rejoined Victor and her brother and found both men sporting heavy cloaks. " 'Tis a good thing the mornings still merit such protection," she said, pulling the cloak around her.

"We must hurry," Victor told her. "We have a bit of distance to cover before we reach our shelter."

"Then let us be gone."

≈

Hours later, after weaving their way behind many establishments along the dock, Jeanine, Victor, and Étienne made their way to a small run-down inn. It wasn't until they were given a single room on the upper floor that Jeanine suddenly thought of her mother and father.

"Étienne, what of our parents?" she questioned, concern clearly evident in her voice. She threw off the cloak and turned to face her brother.

"They are safe," he assured her. "Simon has taken them to another of your patients' homes."

"My patients?" Jeanine grinned. "You mean Dr. Font's patients, no doubt."

Étienne looked at her and shook his head. "It was you on the *Crispin,* was it not?"

She remembered that moment clearly. Fear for Étienne's safety had caused her to place herself in jeopardy of being discovered. "*Oui.* It was I."

"I cannot believe it," Étienne replied. "I did not even know you."

"That was the idea," Jeanine admitted.

"I feel the fool," he said, chuckling.

Victor had gone to the window to check the alleyway behind the inn. "*You* feel the fool?" he called over his shoulder. "The woman worked on me as a physician, and I thought she was a man."

"I am very good at what I do," Jeanine said, feeling the joy of her freedom for the first time. "I like to believe my patients were more focused on being healed than on my ash-stained face and hands."

"Still, it should have been evident," Victor said, coming up behind her.

"Mayhap God clouded your eyes," she offered lightly.

"Whatever the way," Étienne said, still amazed, " 'tis good that you used your abilities, for elsewise, this man would be dead."

Jeanine turned and beheld the look of affection in Victor's eyes. " 'Twould have been my death as well. For my heart scarce beats, but what it thinks of him."

Noises outside the door caused both men to put a finger to Jeanine's lips. It would have been amusing to her, had their looks not have been so grave. The rousing protest of the landlord instantly alerted them to danger. Étienne pulled Jeanine one way, while Victor pulled her the other. Finding herself torn in two different directions, Jeanine hardly knew what to do. She couldn't cry out, and yet to stand in place would see her gravely injured.

The men seemed not to notice, until the voices moved down the hall and they each turned to see why their progress was halted. Jeanine stood, arms outstretched, one man at the end of each tightly held hand.

"Shall you make a wish and cleave me in two?" she asked in a hushed whisper.

Étienne was the first to let go. He laughed very softly and shrugged. "With her father, I've been her protector for a score of years. Old habits are difficult to put aside."

Victor nodded. "I have been blessed by your aid in keeping her from harm. It seems she is one of those people who requires many keepers."

"I take offense at such talk," Jeanine protested. "I've managed to see to myself lo these many years while working on the docks. You have no faith in my abilities."

Victor grinned, and Étienne chuckled. "We have a great

amount of faith in your ability to get yourself into trouble," her brother assured her. He bowed low and made a sweeping movement with his arm. "I give her gladly to you, monsieur. You will never know a moment's peace."

"Mayhap you are right," Victor admitted, "but 'tis my belief she will make up for that loss in other ways."

"Mayhap I will throw you both over for someone else entirely," Jeanine said, crossing her arms against her chest. "I am hardly a woman to be considered lightly. I have a strong faith and a powerful Father in heaven who listens to my cries. Should you think to abuse me overmuch, I will simply put it to Him to be dealt with."

"Let it always be so," Victor said, reaching out to pull her into his arms. "It is my deepest wish that I might never abuse the love and faith you have put in me."

Jeanine relished the way his arms closed around her. She felt safe here. Secure from the worries of the world, and even though she still had far to go in order to reach true safety, she was happy here.

❧

The following morning a light rapping at the door sent Victor hurrying to pull the sleeping form of his wife-to-be from her peaceful slumber on the tiny bed. He and Étienne had slept at the side of the bed on the wood floor and had positioned themselves so that they blocked any hope of entrance should someone try the door.

Jeanine gazed about sleepily, as if to discern what was happening as Victor pushed her down to the floor and silently drew his sword. The rapping came again, and her eyes widened in fear. Victor pressed a finger to his lips and motioned her to remain hidden, while Étienne went to the door.

"Who disturbs my slumber?" he called out in a gruff manner.

" 'Tis only I," came an ancient-sounding voice. "I have brought you food to break the fast."

Jeanine instantly sat back up. " 'Tis Simon," she said in a whisper.

Victor nodded to Étienne and remained fixed with sword, while the younger man opened the door. It was indeed Simon, and he had managed to come alone.

They hurried him into the privacy of their room and quickly shut the door. Jeanine got up from her hiding place and came to embrace the old man. "I do not know when I have found more pleasure in a visitor. Simon, I am so grateful God spared your life."

"As am I," Simon admitted and handed a cloth-wrapped parcel to Victor.

"So what word have you for us?" Étienne asked.

"They are searching for you, as is to be expected. There are criers on the streets announcing your escape, as well as the charges that stand against your sister." He turned to Jeanine with an expression of sorrow. "They still mean to see you dead."

Jeanine nodded. "We knew it would be so."

" 'Tis madness," Simon replied. "They have listened to no one but the devil himself. You will be sorely missed when you are gone from this place. The people love you well."

"Most do not even know I exist," Jeanine protested. "I posed as a male physician. Dr. Font is who they love."

Simon smiled. "They now know well the true identify of Dr. Font. I have spread the word that they might know and realize what has become of their good doctor."

"And they were not offended by the fact that I am a woman?" she asked, taking a piece of hard cheese and bread that Victor offered her.

"You prevented their deaths, nursed their sick children,

brought new lives into the world—they scarce seemed concerned that you were not as you appeared."

"They are good people," Jeanine replied before sinking her teeth hungrily into the cheese.

"Are the plans we made going to work?" Victor asked suddenly.

"At this point, all looks well," Simon assured him.

"What of the men who aided our escape?"

"They escaped without a single death. Two men were injured severely, but I saw to their needs and they now await your escape from Bruges."

"And no one suspects who they were?" Victor questioned. His worst fears were that those men might be found out for who they really were.

"*Non,*" Simon answered. "Colbert has everyone believing that Jeanine summoned up some evil force. Even the bishop is convinced that it must be so, especially when there was no man left behind to prove the human natures of their attackers."

"So Colbert lives?" Étienne asked.

"*Oui,* but his wounds are grieving him greatly, I've been told. He swears a legion of demons attacked him as he tried to bring Jeanine back to her just punishment. The men who were with him at the time of his injury completely agree with this story. They have done much to spread the story of an army of evil."

"But I do not understand," Jeanine said, pausing in her eating to question Victor. "You told me those men were from the king. Was not their standard visible to the bishop and Colbert?"

Victor looked upward for a moment and let out a deep breath. " 'Tis true they are the king's men. I simply left out the matter of *which* king they served."

"You mean to tell me—"

Victor gave her a sly smile and bit off a chunk of bread. He chewed it very thoughtfully before replying. "My family stands well with the king of England. He thought it rather amusing to do something so irritating to old crazy Charlie."

"The king of England sent men to rescue me?" Jeanine said in an air of disbelief. "Why did you not tell me before now?"

"It seemed not to be of importance," Victor replied as if what had been accomplished on her behalf had been less than significant.

"Not of grave importance? The king of England sends his men to Flanders to interfere with the edict of the church, and you think it not of grave importance?" She appeared quite indignant, and Victor could no longer lead her the merry chase.

"I didn't say that the rescue wasn't of importance. I merely meant to imply that *where* our help came from wasn't as important as the fact that it came. Then, too, it was of great import to keep the identity of those men secret. They appeared as mere working men rising up to aid the cause of one of their own. They are safely awaiting us on a ship which sails for England tonight. If all goes as planned, you and I and your family, as well as Simon, if he will come, will be on that ship when it leaves Bruges."

Jeanine stared at him in wonder. "You worked out the details of all this? On my behalf?" Tears filled her eyes.

"Well, I could hardly allow Colbert to deny me of a wife before I even had a chance to ask for her hand in marriage."

Jeanine looked at him with such love and admiration that Victor thought his heart would burst. All his life he had sought to find satisfaction in his work. With his imagination, he designed fine buildings. With his purpose and direction, he was able to hire good men to help him transfer those dreams from paper to stone and mortar. But in the twinkling of an eye, this young woman had given him the satisfaction and fulfillment that had somehow evaded his life.

"I know not what to say," Jeanine said softly and wiped at her eyes with the edge of her sleeve.

"You might agree to marry me," Victor said, reaching his hand up to touch her wet cheek.

"But who will marry me to anyone?" Jeanine asked quite seriously. "The church has branded me a heretic and a witch."

"Trust God to find a way," Victor told her. "He has yet to let us down, eh?" She nodded. "So does that mean you will marry me?"

"Oui," she whispered softly. "I will marry you."

Victor smiled and threw a glance at Étienne and Simon. "See? You rescue the fair damsels and they will happily give themselves over to you in marriage."

Étienne laughed. "But what of the man whose life is saved by a woman?"

Victor sobered and gently stroked Jeanine's cheek. "You lose your heart forever to a woman like that. For you see, she not only saves the body from death, but she saves the heart as well."

eighteen

"But why will you not come with us?" Jeanine asked Simon for the third time. "You are not safe here in Bruges."

"I know that full well," Simon admitted, "and it is not my intention to stay in Bruges. I seek only to see you safely away, and then I will see my own pilgrimage realized."

"Where will you go?" Jeanine asked, barely able to hold back her tears.

"I will return to my homeland to the east," Simon said solemnly. "I long to see what family of mine might still exist there. I have a brother and two sisters, and together they have many children—maybe even grandchildren by now. I desire to see them again before I die."

"Speak not of death. I had thought to have lost you once before, and now it seems I am losing you in truth," Jeanine said, reaching out to touch Simon's shoulder. "You are a dear friend. I know our faith is different, but I will pray for you to reach your family and to know the joy of being reunited with your loved ones."

"And I will pray that the Lord God of Israel will guide you to a better place—to a homeland where you will not face persecution."

The moonlight shone brightly overhead, and Simon smiled and pointed upward. "Imagine them there," he told her, and Jeanine stared quizzically at the skies.

"Imagine what there?"

"Five geese flying," Simon said with a grin. " 'Tis just as you and your family will be. Five geese fleeing persecution and certain death. Five geese flying to safety and hope."

162

"Oh, Simon," she sobbed and clutched the old man tightly in her arms. "I shall miss you so very much."

"And I will miss you, Dr. Font," Simon told her and stroked her head tenderly.

"I am Dr. Font no longer," Jeanine said with a sigh. She pulled away just as Victor arrived on the dock.

"Come," he told her. "Your parents are safely on board, as is your brother. We must leave now or risk discovery." Jeanine nodded and reluctantly let go of Simon as Victor added, "We've still room for one more."

Simon shook his head. "*Non*. I am traveling to my family. May it be well with you. Take good care of my little doctor here. She fears she will no longer find a way to practice what she has learned, but I truly doubt she will stand defeated and idle for long."

"So do I," Victor said with a low chuckle.

Simon smiled and nodded. "Godspeed, my friends," he said softly. "Godspeed."

&.

They were some time out to sea when Jeanine, unable to sleep, came up to the main deck. Her life had so completely changed in only a few short months. It was hard to imagine what might come next. She tried not to fear the future, but even Victor couldn't give her decisive answers as to what they might find awaiting them in England. Victor had great confidence in the friendship his family held with the king, but more so, he reminded Jeanine of the kinship they had as Christians with the King of Kings.

Standing at the deck rail, Jeanine stared out to sea. The moonlight reflecting off the still waters made the sea look like polished black glass. The lightest of breezes put wind in their sails, but their ship small and even now the king's men were rowing the ship toward the English shore.

Contemplating her life seemed a sensible thing to do.

Behind her was France, the condemnation of the church, her medical practice, and Antoine Colbert. Before her stood England, the promise of absolution and forgiveness, the hope of marriage to Victor Pindar. *He loves me,* she thought. Suddenly she felt overwhelmed with emotions at the mere thought of Victor going to so much trouble to save her.

The wind picked up a bit, and without warning someone came to stand behind her. She knew it was Victor without turning to look. She felt so sure of him—of his presence, of his love. What a wonder it was and how she thanked God for His goodness in bringing them together.

"What are you doing here?" he asked softly, pulling her against him.

Jeanine reveled in the pleasure of his arms around her. "I thought I might clear my mind," she finally answered.

"And have you?" he whispered against her ear.

Jeanine sighed. "I have."

"And what did you determine in this clearing of your thoughts?"

"How blessed I am," she admitted. "Blessed that in spite of my sin, God brought about good in my life. He put us together, albeit in a very strange way, and He drew from us both the feelings and truths that would forever bind us together."

"We are blessed," Victor agreed and hugged her even more securely to him.

"No matter what my future holds," Jeanine told him softly. "No matter what happens, I will always love you, and I will always thank God for what He has done in bringing you to me."

Victor turned her very gently, and putting his hands to either side of her face, he said, "It will all work out. You must have faith. Just as your geese fly south in the winter and return again in the spring, you must have faith that

God will restore life and happiness to you."

"But I am happy, Victor. I have you. My family is safe, and even Simon will be outside the reach of the punishing hands of Antoine Colbert."

"But you are worried," Victor said, sensing her deepest secret. "I see it in your eyes. I hear it in your voice. I want to take that fear from you. I want to see you happy, free from the burden you carry. Give it to me, Jeanine, and if not to me, then give it to God."

Jeanine sighed. "How can you know me so well in so short a time?"

He smiled and kissed her forehead. " 'Tis the knowledge that love puts upon one's heart. And, 'tis God's way of joining us together as one."

"I pray that may be so."

"It will be," he promised.

The breeze blew up, chilling Jeanine through the thin cloak, but it wasn't for this reason that she trembled. Victor stared down at her with such intensity that she could scarce stand up to the power of his love. He lowered his lips to hers, and when they touched, Jeanine wrapped her arms around Victor's neck and gave herself over to the splendor of his kiss. In his arms, it was easy to imagine that all would be well.

In the distance, Jeanine could hear someone calling out, but she was so lost in Victor's hold that she refused to focus on the words. It was Victor who pulled away and laughed at her dreamy-eyed stare.

"Did you hear that?"

"Ummm, what?"

"Silly little goose of mine," Victor said, laughing. He turned her in his arms again and pointed. "Look there— see the moonlight catching the white cliffs? My home— our home."

Jeanine's breath caught in her throat and tears again came unbidden to her eyes. " 'Tis beautiful."

"Aye, that it is."

Then as if for the first time, Jeanine realized that in England she would not even be able to speak the language. "Victor," she said, desperation edging her voice as she turned abruptly. "I cannot speak English."

Victor laughed lightly, then surprised her as his laughter turned into a hearty roar of delight. "You will hardly be alone," he said, trying to regain his composure. "So if that is your only fear, put it aside and leave it behind you. English was proclaimed the official language less than forty years ago. There are more people speaking French in England than you would imagine. You should feel quite at home."

Jeanine felt her spirits lift. "Truly?"

"Truly. Even my Eleanor prefers French. She says 'tis a fairer language by far than English. So you will find it easy to converse with her, and she will love you just as I do."

They stood in silence for several moments, watching and waiting as the boat drew ever closer to England. Jeanine prayed fervently for the faith to believe, all the while thanking God for His goodness to allow her freedom from the death Antoine Colbert had planned for her.

"Are you still afraid?" Victor's concern was evident in his tone.

Jeanine nodded. "I cannot lie and say I am not. Lies did nothing but harm me in the past. They will have no part in my new life. Aye, I am afraid, but I know too that there is hope and promise in our future. I will not allow fear to take charge of my life, if that is what you think. I only hope that God will direct me in such a way as to make useful my skills. I do so long to help people."

Victor's eyes seemed to twinkle as the moonlight caught them just right. "I believe, my dear Dr. Font, you will have little trouble in that regard. There are always people to be helped."

"*Oui,* but not always do they desire to be helped by one such as me. Women are not often accepted as physicians, and I cannot help but believe this is true even in your homeland."

Victor grinned mischievously. "Perhaps if you were to borrow some of my clothes, and put ashes and mud upon your face, and send out coded messages. . ."

Jeanine laughed merrily as Victor whirled her around. If anyone thought them strange, no one said so.

"We are truly five geese flying," she said when Victor set her down lightly upon the deck. "Flying to another land where we will start anew."

"Flying to freedom and God's future for our lives," Victor added.

"And to our love," Jeanine murmured.

"And to our love," Victor agreed.

epilogue

Jeanine laughed gleefully at the sight of Victor being chased by his nephew. The boy held a very muddy piglet and was quite intent on his uncle sharing in his good find. Lady Eleanor, a graceful, dark-haired woman who appeared to be a miniature of her brother, joined in the laughter at the escapades of her son and brother.

"Marcus will no doubt catch up to him before long," she said, grinning broadly at Jeanine. "And when he does, there is no telling what havoc we shall see."

"Do you suppose the priest will be shocked?" Jeanine questioned, leaning closer to her new sister-in-law. "I mean, having just joined us in matrimony, will he find it difficult to accept that the groom is off frolicking with his nephew, rather than with his bride?"

Eleanor shook her head. "Not Father McKay. He's known Victor since he was a boy. He'll simply see this as accept-able behavior for my brother."

Jeanine smiled and threw Victor a kiss as he narrowly skirted Eleanor's herb garden and made a mad dash for the garden wall. The pig squealed in terror as Marcus fairly flew by, jumping up and over the end of the Eleanor's favorite roses.

"Truce! Truce!" Victor demanded from atop the garden wall. "I yield to your mercy, Sir Marcus."

The boy laughed at his uncle's ridiculously overdrama-tized bow and put the frightened piglet on the ground. "I could have caught you."

"And well I know it," declared Victor. "Which is precisely

why I yielded the fight. 'Twould do me little good to come to my bride smelling of the pigsty."

"But that is exactly why Étienne told me to do it," Marcus giggled. "He thought it would be a great joke."

Victor jumped down from the wall and caught Jeanine's laughing expression. "No doubt he did, and I can imagine a few great jokes we might yet play on Étienne."

Eleanor was the one to put an end to the conspiratorial glances Victor and Marcus shared. "Not today. Today is for Jeanine's pleasure and goodwill. Today we celebrate the king's declaration of her absolution from the charges of witchcraft and heresy." She paused and added, "As well as your marriage, in case you forgot."

Victor rubbed Marcus lightly on the head and strode toward his sister with determined purpose. "That is not likely." He kissed Eleanor on the cheek, then left her to tend her son while he walked on to where Jeanine stood watching him.

Jeanine's laughter died in her throat as he seriously, passionately fixed his stare on her. He said not a word as he swung her up into his arms and headed for the small castle keep that monopolized the Bramston estate.

"Victor, you can't run away with her just now," Eleanor called after them, and Jeanine giggled at the expression on her husband's face.

"Just watch me," he replied, never breaking his stride.

"Victor!" Eleanor demanded his attention.

He turned on the steps of the keep and grinned mischievously down at his bride. "They will plague us all day and night, if we allow them to." Then to his sister he replied, "Go tend to your party. We will make our own."

"You cannot just leave like this," Eleanor said, coming forward. "What will I tell her family?"

Just then Étienne rounded the corner to catch sight of

the scene. "What goes here?"

Eleanor looked up hopefully. "You must stop him. My brother is acting quite uncivilized."

" 'Tis nothing uncivilized at all," Victor answered them, and winked down at Jeanine. "I merely feel the need for a doctor."

"If that is the case, mayhap she should be carrying you," Étienne said with a laugh, and everyone joined in.

Jeanine had never known such happiness as when she was in Victor's arms, and she trembled at the thought of the passion they shared for one another. She prayed that their marriage would be good, and she hoped that if it were at all possible, her *grandmère* might know of her happiness. Gently she fingered the brooch of sapphires and rubies which Victor had returned to her, along with her grandmother's combs, only the night before. *Perhaps Grandmère does know,* Jeanine thought happily.

Suddenly five geese appeared on the horizon and made a steady flight to the north. "Look!" Jeanine gasped in disbelief. "Victor, look!"

The gathering grew silent and stared heavenward as the birds, ever mindless of their human audience, journeyed past the keep. Victor grinned down at Jeanine, and she knew he understood the meaning of the sight in full. Five geese flying was a sign, her *grandmère* had assured her not so very long ago. A sign of hope—a sign of love.

A Letter To Our Readers

Dear Reader:

In order that we might better contribute to your reading enjoyment, we would appreciate your taking a few minutes to respond to the following questions. When completed, please return to the following:

Rebecca Germany, Managing Editor
Heartsong Presents
P.O. Box 719
Uhrichsville, Ohio 44683

1. Did you enjoy reading *Five Geese Flying?*
   ❑ Very much. I would like to see more books
     by this author!
   ❑ Moderately
     I would have enjoyed it more if _____

   _____

2. Are you a member of **Heartsong Presents**? ❑Yes ❑No
   If no, where did you purchase this book?_____

   _____

3. What influenced your decision to purchase this
   book? (Check those that apply.)

   ❑ Cover   ❑ Back cover copy

   ❑ Title   ❑ Friends

   ❑ Publicity   ❑ Other_____

4. How would you rate, on a scale from 1 (poor) to 5
   (superior), the cover design?_____

5. On a scale from 1 (poor) to 10 (superior), please rate
   the following elements.

   ___Heroine   ___Plot

   ___Hero   ___Inspirational theme

   ___Setting   ___Secondary characters

6. What settings would you like to see covered in
   Heartsong Presents books?_____

   _____

   _____

7. What are some inspirational themes you would like
   to see treated in future books?_____

   _____

   _____

8. Would you be interested in reading other **Heartsong
   Presents** titles?   ❏ Yes   ❏ No

9. Please check your age range:
   ❏ Under 18   ❏ 18-24   ❏ 25-34
   ❏ 35-45   ❏ 46-55   ❏ Over 55

10. How many hours per week do you read? _____

Name _____
Occupation _____
Address _____
City_____ State_____ Zip_____

·········· Presents ··········

___HP211 MY VALENTINE, *Tracie J.*
         Peterson
___HP215 TULSA TRESPASS, *Norma Jean Lutz*
___HP216 BLACK HAWK'S FEATHER,
         Carolyn R. Scheidies
___HP219 A HEART FOR HOME, *Norene*
         Morris
___HP220 SONG OF THE DOVE, *Peggy Darty*
___HP223 THREADS OF LOVE, *Judith*
         McCoy Miller
___HP224 EDGE OF DESTINY, *Darlene*
         Mindrup
___HP227 BRIDGET'S BARGAIN, *Loree Lough*
___HP228 FALLING WATER VALLEY, *Mary*
         Louise Colln
___HP235 THE LADY ROSE, *Joyce Williams*
___HP236 VALIANT HEART, *Sally Laity*
___HP239 LOGAN'S LADY, *Tracie J. Peterson*

___HP240 THE SUN STILL SHINES, *Linda Ford*
___HP243 THE RISING SUN, *Darlene Mindrup*
___HP244 WOVEN THREADS, *Judith McCoy*
         Miller
___HP247 STRONG AS THE REDWOOD,
         Kristin Billerbeck
___HP248 RETURN TO TULSA, *Norma Jean*
         Lutz
___HP251 ESCAPE ON THE WIND, *Jane*
         LaMunyon
___HP252 ANNA'S HOPE, *Birdie L. Etchison*
___HP255 KATE TIES THE KNOT, *Loree Lough*
___HP256 THE PROMISE OF RAIN, *Sally*
         Krueger
___HP259 FIVE GEESE FLYING, *Tracie*
         Peterson
___HP260 THE WILL AND THE WAY,
         DeWanna Pace

Great Inspirational Romance at a Great Price!

Heartsong Presents books are inspirational romances in contemporary and historical settings, designed to give you an enjoyable, spirit-lifting reading experience. You can choose wonderfully written titles from some of today's best authors like Peggy Darty, Sally Laity, Tracie Peterson, Colleen L. Reece, Lauraine Snelling, and many others.

When ordering quantities less than twelve, above titles are $2.95 each.
Not all titles may be available at time of order.

Hearts♥ng Presents
Love Stories Are Rated G!

That's for godly, gratifying, and of course, great! If you love a thrilling love story, but don't appreciate the sordidness of some popular paperback romances, **Heartsong Presents** is for you. In fact, **Heartsong Presents** is the *only inspirational romance book club*, the only one featuring love stories where Christian faith is the primary ingredient in a marriage relationship.

Sign up today to receive your first set of four, never before published Christian romances. Send no money now; you will receive a bill with the first shipment. You may cancel at any time without obligation, and if you aren't completely satisfied with any selection, you may return the books for an immediate refund!

Imagine. . .four new romances every four weeks—two historical, two contemporary—with men and women like you who long to meet the one God has chosen as the love of their lives. . .all for the low price of $9.97 postpaid.

To join, simply complete the coupon below and mail to the address provided. **Heartsong Presents** romances are rated G for another reason: They'll arrive *Godspeed!*